Two decades ago, under the pen name Randy Striker, the New York Times bestselling author wrote this macho thriller classic. . . .

PRAISE FOR RANDY WAYNE WHITE AND HIS NOVELS

"What James Lee Burke has done for Louisiana, Tony Hillerman for the Southwest, John Sandford for Minnesota, and Joe R. Lansdale for east Texas, Randy Wayne White does for his own little acre."
—*Chicago Tribune*

"White take us places that no other Florida mystery writer can hope to find." —*Carl Hiaasen*

"White brings vivid imagination to his fight scenes. Think Mickey Spillane meets *The Matrix*." —*People*

"A major new talent . . . hits the ground running . . . a virtually perfect piece of work. He's the best new writer we've encountered since Carl Hiaasen."
—*The Denver Post*

"White is the rightful heir to joining John D. MacDonald, Carl Hiaasen, James Hall, Geoffrey Norman. . . . His precise prose is as fresh and pungent as a salty breeze." —*The Tampa Tribune*

"White doesn't just use Florida as a backdrop, but he also makes the smell, sound and physicality of the state leap off the page." —*South Florida Sun-Sentinel*

Key West
CONNECTION

Randy Wayne White

writing as Randy Striker

A SIGNET BOOK

SIGNET
Published by New American Library, a division of
Penguin Group (USA) Inc., 375 Hudson Street,
New York, New York 10014, USA
Penguin Group (Canada), 90 Eglinton Avenue East, Suite 700, Toronto,
Ontario M4P 2Y3, Canada (a division of Pearson Penguin Canada Inc.)
Penguin Books Ltd., 80 Strand, London WC2R 0RL, England
Penguin Ireland, 25 St. Stephen's Green, Dublin 2,
Ireland (a division of Penguin Books Ltd.)
Penguin Group (Australia), 250 Camberwell Road, Camberwell, Victoria 3124,
Australia (a division of Pearson Australia Group Pty. Ltd.)
Penguin Books India Pvt. Ltd., 11 Community Centre, Panchsheel Park,
New Delhi - 110 017, India
Penguin Group (NZ), cnr Airborne and Rosedale Roads, Albany,
Auckland 1310, New Zealand (a division of Pearson New Zealand Ltd.)
Penguin Books (South Africa) (Pty.) Ltd., 24 Sturdee Avenue,
Rosebank, Johannesburg 2196, South Africa

Penguin Books Ltd., Registered Offices:
80 Strand, London WC2R 0RL, England

Published by Signet, an imprint of New American Library,
a division of Penguin Group (USA) Inc.

First Printing with Introduction by Author, April 2006

10 9 8 7 6 5 4 3 2 1

To Scooter and Lee Wayne

". . . and they died with the smiles on their faces."

WILLIE NELSON

Introduction

In the winter of 1980, I received a surprising phone call from an editor at Signet Books—surprising because, as a Florida fishing guide, the only time New Yorkers called me was to charter my boat. And if any of my clients were editors, they were savvy enough not to admit it.

The editor said she'd read a story by me in *Outside Magazine* and was impressed. Did I have time to talk?

As a mediocre high school jock, my idols were writers, not ball players. I had a dream job as a light-tackle guide, yet I was still obsessed with my own dream of writing for a living. For years, before and after charters, I'd worked hard at the craft. Selling a story to *Outside*, one of the country's finest publications, was a huge break. I was about to finish a novel, but this was the first time New York had called.

Yes, I had time to talk.

The editor, whose name was Joanie, told me Signet wanted to launch a paperback thriller series that featured a recurring he-man hero. "We want at least four writers on the project because we want to keep the books coming, publishing one right after the other, to create momentum."

Four writers producing books with the same character?

"Characters," Joanie corrected. "Once we get going, the cast will become standard."

Signet already had a template for the hero. He was a Vietnam vet turned Key West fishing guide, she said, talking as if the man existed. He was surfer-boy blond, and he'd been friends with Hemingway.

I am not a literary historian, but all my instincts told me the timetable seemed problematic. I said nothing.

"He has a shark scar," Joanie added, "and he's freakishly strong. Like a man who lifts weights all the time."

The guys I knew who lifted weights were also reakishly clumsy, so . . . maybe the hero, while visiting a local aquarium, tripped during feeding time?

My brain was already problem-solving.

"He lives in Key West," she said, "so, of course, he has to be an expert on the area. That's why I'm calling. You live in Key West, and I liked your magazine story a lot. It seems like a natural fit."

Actually, I fished out of Sanibel Island, on Florida's Gulf Coast, a six hour drive from Sloppy Joe's, but this was no time for petty details.

"Have you ever been to Key West?" I asked the editor. "Great sunsets."

Editors, I have since learned, can also be cagey. Joanie didn't offer me the job. She had already settled on three of the four writers, she said, but if I was willing to submit a few sample chapters on speculation, she'd give me serious consideration.

Money? A contract? That stuff was "all standard," she told me, and could be discussed later.

"I'll warn you right now," she said, "there are a

couple of other writer we're considering, so you need to get at least three chapters to me within a month. Then I'll let you know."

I hung up the phone, stunned by my good fortune. My first son, Lee, had been born only a few months earlier. My much adored wife, Debra, and I were desperate for money because the weather that winter had been miserable for fishing. But it was *perfect* for writing.

I went to my desk, determined not to let my young family down.

At Tarpon Bay Marina, where I was a guide, my friend Ralph Woodring owned a boat with *Dusky* painted in big blue letters on the side. My friend, Graeme Mellor, lived on a Morgan sailboat named *No Mas*.

Dusky MacMorgan was born.

Every winter, Clyde Beatty-Cole Bros. Circus came to town. Their trapeze artists, I realized, were not only freakishly strong, but they were also freakishly nimble.

Dusky gathered depth.

One of my best friends was the late Dr. Harold Westervelt, a gifted orthopedic surgeon. Dr. Westervelt became the Edison of Death, and he loved introducing himself that way to new patients. His son, David, became Westy O'Davis, and our spearfishing pal, Billy, became Billy Mack.

Problems with my hero's shark scar and his devoted friendship with Hemingway were also solved.

Working around the clock, pounding away at my old black manual typewriter, I wrote *Key West Connection* in nine days. On a Monday morning, I waited for the post office to open to send it to New York.

Joanie sounded a little dazed when she telephoned on Friday. Was I willing to try a second book on spec?

Hell, yes.

God, I was beginning to *love* New York's can-do attitude.

The other three writers (if they ever existed) were fired, and I became to sole proprietor of Capt. Dusky MacMorgan—although Signet owned the copyright and all other rights after I signed Joanie's "standard" contract. (This injustice was later made right by a willing and steadfast publisher and my brilliant agent.)

If Joanie (a fine editor) feels badly about that today, she shouldn't. I would've signed for less.

I wrote seven of what I would come to refer to as "duck and fuck" books because in alternating chapters Dusky would duck a few bullets, then spend much-deserved time alone with a heroine.

Seldom did a piece of paper go into my old typewriter that was ripped out and thrown away, and I suspect that's the way the books read. I don't know. I've never reread them. I do remember using obvious clichés, a form of self-loathing, as if to remind myself that I should be doing my *own* writing, not this job-of-work.

The book you are now holding, and the other six, constituted a training arena for a young writer who took seriously the discipline demanded by his craft and also the financial imperatives of being a young father.

For years, I apologized for these books. I no longer do.

—Randy Wayne White
Cartagena, Colombia

1

We were out at the edge of the Gulf Stream, trolling for the big ones, when I got word that my best friend was dead.

I was up on the fighting deck boning a six-inch silver mullet—an ideal sailfish bait—when my Konel VHF-780 marine radio started squawking at me. It was Nels Chester of the *Southern Cross II*, a fellow charter captain out of Key West. I went below, adjusted the squelch, and took the mike.

"This is the *Sniper*. This is the *Sniper*. What's up, Nels?"

"Oh Christ, Dusky. Jesus. I don't know how to . . ."

Even over the VHF I could tell that his voice was choked with emotion. The first thing that crossed my mind was that there was something wrong with my wife, Janet, or one of my twin boys, Ernest and Honor.

"Get hold of yourself, goddammit, Nels. Give it to me straight."

"Dusky, they got him. They got Billy Mack. He was out here 'bout a mile or two from me. Fishin' for dolphin. They hijacked his boat, Dusky. And they killed him. Slit his throat. Oh, Christ. I found him floatin' just now. . . ."

"Shut up, Nels! Listen to me!" My heart was pounding loud in my ears, the adrenaline roaring through my body like a drug. "What kind of boat were they in? And which way did they take off?"

Nels was starting to regain a little control. "There were four of them, Dusky. Two black guys, two white. In one of those racing boats. Cigarette hull. Dark-blue. Saw them through my binoculars, heading Billy Mack's way. Then I got a call from Billy Mack. Said he was going to the aid of a disabled power vessel. I knew goddam well there was something funny about that. I watched them, Dusky. I watched them climb up on his boat, all thank-yous and appreciation, then the biggest black guy got behind him, and I saw the knife, Dusky, but there was nothing I could do, I swear! I saw it all through the binoculars. Oh, lordy, lordy, he's layin' on my deck now like he's got two mouths; one with this bloody awful smile on it. . . ."

So they had killed him. Killed my best friend. Billy Mack. We had served three tours together in Nam. The United States Navy. SEALS. The best of the best, the toughest of the tough, and if you know anything at all about the Navy's Underwater Demolition

Team—especially the exclusive branch of SEALS—
you would know that we are all closer than brothers.
The Brotherhood of Hell, that's what our old chief
called it. Once, when Billy Mack and I were in the
first round of training, out in Coronado, just kids,
really, trying to win our fins, they had come to our
barracks at three a.m. And they ran us all out into
the Pacific seven miles.

"See those lights?" our chief said, pointing to the
faint blaze of lights over the California mainland.
"You maggots swim to breakfast. And if you're late
for chow call, you don't eat."

We had no lights, no moon, no fins, no nothing.
Billy Mack was just a farm boy from a place called
Kunkle, Ohio. A tough little guy, but scared to death
of swimming at night. Later, in Nam, when we pa-
trolled the harbors every night underwater, we
laughed about it. But back then he was scared shit-
less. He stuck close to me. In fact, everybody stuck
close to me. I was their leader; leader without rank,
but I knew everyone depended on me. I was the
biggest, the fastest, the strongest. I think even the
chief was a little afraid of me. One time I overheard
him talking with the OIC:

"Jesus Christ, have you had a look at that Henry
MacMorgan kid? Looks like he was built out of four-
by-sixes. And his shoulders—like some kinda freak
or somethin'. Must be four feet wide across the goddamn back. You see that blond hair, that little angel
kid's face of his, and you figure he oughtta be in the
back seat of a Dodge copping feels off some high

school girl. But then you get a look at those eyes—kinda battleship-gray they are—and you know, you just know he ain't gonna balk when it comes his turn to kill."

"I got the dope on him," the OIC had said. "Strange case. He was an orphan. Raised in the circus by an Italian family that worked the trapeze. That's where he got those shoulders. Seems they were playin' some small town and some local toughs thought it would be funny to cut a rope here and there and watch the big top tent fall. Happened right in the middle of their act. Everyone was killed but MacMorgan. He caught up with those toughs. I don't know what he did, but it musta been nasty. When he got here the federal boys were hot on his tail. They said, 'You take him or else.' We pretended like we didn't know that he lied about his age. You know how old he is? Sixteen goddamn years old. I wouldn't get on his bad side, if I were you, Skip. After this training, he's going to be one thoroughly dangerous SOB."

So they dropped us seven miles off in the Pacific. A hot August night and back on the mainland other kids our age were riding the one-ways in their hopped-up cars and listening to the Beach Boys, planning their surfing parties. We stuck close together, heading toward shore in a tight V. Just when we thought we had it licked, only a mile or two from shore, that's when the shark moved in, throwing up a big green glowing wake of bioluminescence. We knew it was a shark by the way it circled, and we knew it was huge by the force of the wake.

Everyone started to panic. Billy Mack was going wild, screaming at it, kicking at it madly. I grabbed him by the hair and jerked his ear up to my lips. I whispered hoarsely:

"Listen, you stupid farm-boy bastard. If that shark kills us he kills us. But if he doesn't kill us, you can bet these guys are gonna remember how you acted. And they ain't ever gonna respect you. Never. And you'd be *better off* being dead, I can guarantee you that."

It settled him better than a slap in the face. The shark's circles were getting tighter and tighter. I knew our only chance was to try to scare it off. I pulled my knife from the scabbard belted to my calf; the good Randall attack-survival model 18; the one with the seven-and-a-half-inch blade of the finest stainless made, the one with the threaded brass butt cap and waterproof O-ring, and flared holes in the hilt for converting it to a spear. That knife had cost me a month's pay, and now I was going to see if it was worth it. I moved out away from the V, thrashing my arms, trying to set myself up as bait. Strangely, I wasn't surprised to see Billy Mack right beside me. If I was going to be bait then, dammit, he was going to be bait too. A tough little guy. On the shark's first pass, I expected to be bumped. That's the way it happens in the survival books they had pounded into our heads. A shark first bumps, *then* circles back to attack. But this was the deep-water Pacific. At night. And this shark wasn't a member of any literary guild. I felt no pain, only impact. It was like being dragged behind a ski boat without skis. Water was being forced up my nose, my face contorted by our speed through the water. Somehow, I got around behind the shark, holding onto his back for dear life. Only I knew I was already a dead man. He was too big for me to get my arms clear around him, and I thought: This is one magnificent son of a bitch. Again and again I stabbed that fish, probing for its heart with that good Randall knife. I tried to remember my shark anatomy: over 250 species; single circulation system, phylum Vertebrata, no true bone cells, skeletal support from cartilage, tiny cordlike brain—none of that information was worth a damn. What I did know was this: sharks, like some people, die very very hard. The shark began to sound, swimming toward the bottom. I didn't care. In that black underwater world, all I knew was that I was going to kill that shark or die trying. My air was gone. Funny colors, red and green and yellow, exploded in my brain. With one last great effort, I buried the knife in the shark's underbelly and pulled with all my strength, trying to slice clear to the anal cavity. I felt the huge shudder, felt that great fish list sideways in its final, convulsive, circular death dance.

I don't know how I made it back to the surface. But I did. Billy Mack was still there. The rest of the guys were a couple hundred yards away, trying to make it to land. I didn't blame them. Later, each and every one of them would risk their lives—and some would, in the end, lose their lives—for me.

"Jesus Christ," Billy Mack had said, amazed that I was still among the breathing. "You were down there *forever*. For goddam *forever*. I thought . . . I thought . . ."

There was an odd, burning sensation around my left pelvic area. "Billy Mack," I told him, gasping, beginning to cramp with pain, "as long as I'm around, you ain't ever gonna die. And as long as you're around, I ain't gonna die. Remember that, buddy. I'm hurt, Billy. Maybe bad. You gotta get me back. Promise me that. You won't let me die, I won't let you die."

It took 148 stitches. It was a huge dusky shark—they knew from a ragged tooth imbedded in my pelvis. Forever afterward, I was known as "Dusky."

"Very rare," the Navy marine biologist told me later. "A dusky almost never attacks man and certainly not in the Pacific. It's an Atlantic shark. Until you came along, that is. It's almost a kind of strange privilege. You ought to feel proud, MacMorgan."

And for all these years, I *had* felt a strange pride in it. I had beaten nature's own perfect rogue warrior and gone back for more. When Billy and I got sick and tired of Nam—the politics, the pointless battles governed by pointless little men who never wanted you to win, not really—we retired, went to Key West, started chartering. I met Janet, who was then an actress on location in the Keys. The most beautiful woman I had ever seen, before or since. She told me she was tired of the glamour grind, the parties and premieres, the newspaper clowns always sniffing around. She said all she really wanted out of life was a home, kids, and something else; something that she had discovered was very rare indeed—a real man.

Billy Mack handled the wedding details single-handedly. I hated that sort of crap, and Janet was on location in Ireland: her final film. And when Ernest and Honor came along he was official godfather and legal guardian if anything happened. They never tired of listening to his stories. Especially the story about the big dusky.

"Tell us again how Daddy got his name, Uncle Billy," they would beg him.

Billy Mack and I wanted to get old and slack and slow together. He had his stories and I had that wide indentation of scar on my pelvis: the symbol of a promise we had made each other a long, long time ago one night in the black Pacific.

But now, four strangers had made a liar out of me. Two black guys, two white, in a ritzy racing boat. I had been around, and I had let Billy Mack die. And now someone was going to pay.

II

"Dusky! Dusky! Are you listenin'?"

The reality of Nels Chester screaming at me over the Konel VHF jolted me out of my nostalgic reverie.

"Yeah, I'm here, Nels."

"Christ, I thought for a second they'd gotten you too."

"Not hardly. Tell me again: which way were they headed?"

"Well, east-nor'east, tryin' to pick up the main shippin' markers into Key West, I suppose. But if you're figurin' on interceptin' that cigarette hull, Dusky, there's just no way, 'cause it's clear outta sight already."

"Shut up, Nels. What about Billy Mack's boat? How many guys are in it?"

"Two. The big colored guy that cut Billy, and one of the white guys."

"That course, Nels—that course will bring them

right by the shoals at Sand Key and Eastern Dry Rocks, won't it?''

"Yeah, but hell, they won't even know those shoals are there. They ain't gonna slow up. I been around boats all my life, and these guys don't know what in the hell they're doin'.''

"One more thing, Nels. Give me half an hour before you notify the Coast Guard.''

"What?''

"Just do it, goddammit! Now, cover up Billy Mack good. Use that white fly-bridge canvas—I'll buy you a new one. And when you get back to the docks, don't let any of those gore seekers or newspapermen stare at him. I won't let them do that to Billy Mack. If I hear that it happened, I'll come looking for you, Nels. You know me; you know I mean it.''

I switched the VHF off in the middle of Nels' indignant protestations, then hurried deckside.

"Fish on!"

The guy who had chartered my boat sat tensed in the chrome-and-white fighting chair while, astern of us, a big Atlantic sailfish, iridescent blue in the black-blue water of the Gulf Stream, knifed its way through the weak trolling chop, mullet bait already in its mouth.

"Thousand *one*. Thousand *two* . . .''

Before he had a chance to finish his count and strike the fish, I had whipped my Gerber fishing knife out and cut the line. His face registered surprise, then outrage.

"What in the hell . . . ? What are you, some kinda

madman?" He jumped out of the fighting chair, letting the big Penn Senator reel fall with a thud onto the deck. He shoved me back against the ladder to the fly bridge of my old custom-built, thirty-four-foot sportsfisherman, hands gripping the collars of my shirt.

I didn't like the guy to begin with. He had chartered me three days in a row, each day coming aboard with the loud and braggartly flourish of the gaudy rich, browbeating his pretty blond wife, lecturing her when she missed her first fish. I couldn't understand it. She was a good woman. A beautiful face and figure; soft weight of breasts lifting full and firm under the denim shirts that she wore. And she was obviously intelligent. Once I caught her looking at me in the soft way that women do when they are interested in a man. And when I caught her, her gaze hardened, softened, then hardened again. She seemed to be saying: "Okay, I made a mistake. I married a bratty man-child who isn't big enough or confident enough to allow his wife to live as an individual. He gropes for integrity by stealing mine, and his ego feeds on making me look small and silly and foolish. I made a mistake, but I'll live with it. I don't need an affair with a big blond hulk of a charterboat captain to salvage what humanity I have left. That would only make me feel even more pathetic. No matter how good-looking you are, no matter how tender you might be. And as much as I would like to. . . ."

His hands tightened, pulling his big hams of fists

up under my chin when he realized how easily he had shoved me back against the ladder.

"I want my money back, *Captain* MacMorgan. Every goddam cent of it. That was my one shot at a trophy fish, and you blew it. It could have been a world's record on thirty-pound, and I want a refund. *Now!*"

He was a big guy. A whole head taller than I am— and I'm just a tad over six feet two. The college full-back type; maybe tight end. If so, that had been some years and twenty pounds ago. Oh, in a fight, he might even now have been able to summon all that strength and speed of college days—but not for more than forty seconds. And, frankly, I didn't give a shit if he could. Slowly, ever so slowly, I reached up and took his wrist in my right hand, and then began to squeeze. Softly at first. Then harder. I watched his face. First, he was amused. Then surprised. And then his face blanched white with pain. I felt the small carpal bone pop and crush beneath my grip.

"Oh, Jesus!" His hands fell limply to his sides. "Jesus, you broke my . . ."

Gently, I grabbed his shirt collar and swung him into the cabin, noticing, as I did, the slightest of wry smiles on the face of his wife.

"Listen to me, fat boy," I said in a hoarse whisper. "And listen good. In about ten minutes I've got a very important date with a couple of murderers. It won't take long. And I want you and that nice woman—I'm not going to call her your wife because that implies ownership, and she's too good to be owned by anybody, especially you—to do what I say. You lock yourselves in the head and don't come out no matter what you hear."

"You're crazy," the big man said, eyes wide with horror. "I refuse to be a part of any of it. I demand you take us back to Key West immediately. I demand . . . hey, what are you doing?"

I had lowered him down into a booth seat beside the galley. I was rummaging around in the food locker and finally found what I was looking for. A little tin of Copenhagen snuff. I held it up.

"See this stuff? Got hooked on it when I was a kid in the circus. I was a catch man—the best, some used to say. But there was a lot of pressure, lot of responsibility. Got so before each show I had to have a dip of this Copenhagen. Then, in Vietnam, I had it shipped over. Couldn't fight without it; that's how it got to be. I killed seventeen men in hand-to-hand combat *above* water, and the last thing thirteen of them saw was me about to spit this shit into their eyes. Now, do you have some idea of what I'm doing?"

There was a wild look of terror in his eyes. He made a lunge for the VHF. I caught him in midstride, swung him around, and slapped him; four good stingers.

"Okay," he said, a little whimper escaping. "Okay, I'll do anything you say."

"Good. Just lock yourselves in the head and don't come out. No matter what."

I started up deckside, then stopped and turned

around. His chubby face was pallid and he was holding his wrist. I said, "Your wife didn't see any of this. So it never happened as far as I'm concerned. If she had seen you humiliated, I know what you would have done. Taken it all out on her. Made her life an even bigger hell than it is right now. So forget it. Right?"

He nodded quickly.

I jumped the steps to topside and came immediately face to face with the woman. I slammed the cabin door behind me.

"You heard?"

She nodded somberly. She seemed to be on the verge of tears, her lovely face flushed, and I realized that I had seen only one prettier woman in my life— Janet, my wife.

"I'm sorry," I said. "I had to do it. My best friend was just . . . just murdered. The guys who did it . . . well. See that light tower toward shore a ways? That's the marker at Sand Key. If my guess is right, they'll skirt Sand Key, turn directly for Western Head and the channel into Key West. And if they do, I've got 'em. They'll go around at Eastern Dry Rocks, or I'll intercept them. Either way, they're dead."

She gasped. In her eyes was sadness and deep concern. "You can't do that, Captain MacMorgan. You have a wife to think about. And you love her; love her very much. I can tell. You're the first man who never . . . never . . ."

"Made a pass at you, Mrs. Johnson?"

She smiled at me then; reached up with a soft dry

hand and touched my face. "Did you really kill seventeen men in hand-to-hand combat?"

"Maybe."

I watched her study my eyes.

"Yes, I think you did, Captain MacMorgan." She stood on tiptoe and brushed my cheek lightly with her soft lips. For an instant I felt the fullness of nipple and breast against my chest; felt the brief heat of thighs against my leg. "I wish you well, captain. I had forgotten: there are still some men who do the things they have to do. No matter what."

III

Nels Chester was wrong. There weren't two of them. There were three. And when that fatal unknown jammed the phallic muzzle of a .45-caliber service automatic in my back I knew that, in unintentionally breaking my long-ago promise to Billy Mack, I had vanquished all our vows.

On that afternoon, I too would die.

It had started out as such a fine day: old morning sun lifting up over the turquoise expanse of coral sea; rolling its fresh August heat over Crawfish Key, and Mule Key, sweet with the cloying odor of jasmine, right into Key West. As always, I awoke with the first sound of waking birds. My wife, Janet, slept beside me, cool on cotton sheets, long auburn hair and soft nakedness in revolving shadow beneath the ceiling fan.

She stretched, yawned, heavy breasts lifting with each slow inhalation. "Dusky? Do you have to leave already?"

I had nuzzled her face, felt her mouth open to accept the proffered good-morning kiss, felt her legs part as I stripped the cotton sheet away, felt her buttocks lift and rise as my tongue traced the curve of back, reaching deep into the abyss of white thighs, finding the auburn and silken source of my own two sons. I had entered her from behind, then, sliding gently into those well-loved depths. Her nipples flushed, swelled, lengthened; that soft body coming alive as she lay half asleep, eyes closed, wry smile on her face as if we enjoyed the common bond of all secrets of all time. She whimpered, shuddered, gasped, and grew feverish.

"My God, Dusky . . . ah . . . you seemed huge when I met you, and you seem to get bigger . . . ah . . . every year. . . ."

Soft morning giggle of the teenager she would always be; of the vampish lover that the film critics—who had praised her beauty and her acting lavishly—would never know.

Down at the docks, with the smell of freshening sea wind moving over the long white brigade of charter boats, I saw bottlenosed dolphins hunting the flats off Trumbo Point. A good sign. I am a man who looks for good omens and worries about the bad. Superstitious. Like every circus performer on earth. Carlos de Marti, who had trained with me for the Bay of Pigs fiasco, was already on the docks, a long night of dark sea behind him.

"*Hola, mi amigo!*"

"*Buenos días, capitán!*"

"Tu tienes mi cerveza?"

"Sí!"

He helped me load the two cases of excellent Cuban beer aboard the *Sniper*. Once a month, Carlos made the dangerous crossing to Cuba alone, meeting the love of his life on a rural shore of the northern coast, then heading back the next night. Someday he'll be caught. And shot or imprisoned. But for more than two years, once a month, he has brought me back forty-eight rations of that good Hatuey beer. I had learned to love it when I was barely a teenager. It was my first time in Key West, and after our third show, nearly midnight, I had walked down to Mallory Docks alone. And there was Papa, a writer I had loved but never met. Grizzly white beard, whiskey-cask chest, he stood with hands in pockets on the deserted docks, looking out into the midnight sea toward his beloved Cuba. Even then, I was almost as big as he: six feet tall, 185 pounds. The fact that I worked the trapeze interested him. And he came to watch me the next night. And afterward, we went out walking again, through the empty old pirate streets of Key West, down to the docks. With him he carried a huge thermos of beer.

"Old-timer," he had said, "drinking and writing have many similarities yet one great difference. They both make you feel fine, they both should be approached with discipline and respect. But drinking *should* be taught. And writing—good writing—can never ever be taught."

That night he taught me how to drink beer. Good

Hatuey beer. The rest of the world already looked upon him as a living legend. As I did. But that night, standing side by side, looking out into the strangely promising expanse of black sea, I came to look upon him as a friend, too.

So it had been a good morning. A promising morning. Dolphins feeding and a fresh larder of beer.

Until the call. Until Nels Chester told me Billy Mack, my best friend, had been murdered.

Once I had the Johnson couple, alienated man and wife, secured in the head below, I headed for the shoals inside Eastern Dry Rocks. But not before I had taken the Randall knife from its storage place in the starboard locker. That knife was made for two things and two things only. Life. And death. I hadn't worn it in seven years. I took off my belt, took off my shirt, strapped the knife firmly just between armpit and left breast, then put my shirt back on. It wouldn't show. I had a rifle aboard. A Russian assault automatic, an AK-47, fully loaded with 7.62mm cartridges. I had smuggled it back from Nam. I kept it secured horizontally above the forward controls in spring clips. I used it for sharks, the open-ocean sharks that vector in on a hooked billfish. But I didn't want to use it on these guys. You shoot someone down at sea—no matter what they've done—and you end up in court. I wanted to make it look like self-defense. And besides that, I wanted to look into their eyes. I wanted them to know why they were going to die. I wanted their last thoughts to be about Billy Mack.

I had two plans of action. If they went aground on the shoals, I would putter up like a friendly weekend fisherman and offer assistance. If they didn't go aground, I would try to flag them down, pretending I was disabled. And just hope and pray they tried on me what they did to Billy.

I would have no trouble intercepting them. In my thirty-four-foot *Sniper* I had twin 453 GM diesels, and all Billy's old Chris Craft had was a standard-power Caterpillar 3208, single-screw. We used to laugh about the differences between our two boats. His was so slow and sure, mine was so fast and erratic: reflections of our separate personalities. He was by far the better fisherman.

"Hell, Dusky," he had once said, "you ought to fish like me—just hunt around till you find 'em. But no, you can't be that way. You gotta work the long shots; pick a spot an' wait for the big ones to come by. Christ, you fish like a sniper. That's it—a goddamn sniper!"

And so my boat was named.

Key West was a heat mirage on the turquoise slick of open water. A power skiff threw silver wake as it cut across Whitehead Spit, angling inland by old Fort Taylor. I picked up the bell buoy which was Marker 2, skirted the spoil area, then dropped her down and shut her off, drifting on the inside of Eastern Dry Rocks.

I checked my Rolex Submariner watch. If they had followed Nels' predicted course, they should have already been in sight. But they weren't. I was flooded with second thoughts, other possibilities. Why couldn't they just run Southwest Channel toward Key West? No, Nels had said they didn't know boats. They didn't know the water, so they'd head for markers. But why in hell would they be taking a hijacked boat inland anyway? Because that was the only place they could hide it. And as far as they were concerned, no one knew they had slit a good man's throat to get it. Why would anybody be watching for them?

No, I had them. They had to come my way. And the *Sniper* was waiting.

I finally raised them as they moved out from behind Sand Key, Billy's white Chris Craft rolling a glassy blue wake abeam. I could see the name, three feet high, on the port side: *Ernie's Honor;* named after his two godsons, my two boys.

I watched them cut inside, toward Rock Key. They were going to hit it. My breath was coming soft and shallow. I steered with them. Hit it, *please* hit it. Go aground on those shoals!

But they didn't. At the last minute, they noticed the change in the water, or the weak roll of water over the rocks, or looked at their chart or something. Nels was wrong. Someone aboard *Ernie's Honor* knew water. Someone aboard knew boats.

I took a deep breath and moved to start my engines, ready to effect my second plan. I would play disabled, the helpless victim. And that's when I heard the loud *thud*. The submerged pilings! I'd forgotten about them. They'd missed the shoals and hit the pilings! A weird low chuckle escaped from my lips; a ghastly death laugh I thought I had left behind for good in Vietnam. The piling had knocked the prop off *Ernie's Honor*, and with sudden loss water resistance, the old Caterpillar engine screamed like an animal in pain. Finally, someone had the good sense to shut it off. They tried to start it again then shut the scream off again when they realized they weren't going anywhere without a prop.

When they noticed me idling up, one of the two men disappeared into the cabin. It was the black one; Billy's murderer. I would keep that in mind. I moved toward them, smiling broadly, waving every now and then. When I was sure they had drifted free of the pilings, I pulled up along their bow and made my port side fast to the forward bollard with a couple of quick hitches.

The man who stood above me on the bow of Billy's boat was the Nordic type. Blond and angular with a broad Celtic face. He was nervous. His head kept sweeping back and forth, as if scanning to see if there were any witnesses around. He wasn't much past twenty-one. About six feet tall, matted hair down to his shoulders, skinny and emaciated and pallid, as most drug freaks are.

So that was it. Drugs. They'd stolen Billy's boat to make a drug run. Once through, they would probably either sink it or abandon it. It happens all too often in the Florida Keys. Especially around Key West. All the lost ones, the empty-headed young suburbanites, all follow that Southern Highway A1A till it dead-ends abruptly 150 miles out to sea; come to Key West where the drugs are cheap and good and dream their lives away. In the last year, Janet had talked more and more frequently about leaving our little shipbuilder's house of white board and batten on Elizabeth Street, and heading for the rural, unspoiled areas of northern Florida or Georgia. Too many dead-enders in Key West, now. Too many druggies and dead-enders, and empty, empty young people. And she was right. It was no longer Papa's Key West. Nor was it the Key West I had fallen in love with. It was still a pirate town. But the pirates who roamed there now—like the blond kind with the dead eyes who stood before me—were far more dangerous and far less daring than any of the pirates who had lived there before them.

They wanted piracy? I would show them real piracy. The United States government had spent more than a hundred thousand bucks training me, readying me, teaching me how to be far more lethal than the little stubnosed .38 I saw tucked in the back pocket of the kid's dirty jeans. And my piracy wouldn't be one of cold-blooded expediency, one that would barter innocent lives so that drug-induced dreams might be enjoyed. Mine was a piracy of vengeance.

"Havin' a little engine trouble, huh?" I smiled my loosest, friendliest smile.

"What? Oh, yeah, man. Hit somethin'. Really, you

know, bummed me out. Just cruisin' back to Key West an' *whack*." He studied my boat nervously. "You by yourself?"

I acted as if I didn't even notice the abruptness of the question. Still grinning, I reached into my shirt pocket and took out the Copenhagen.

"Want a little dip of this?"

His eyes glowed momentarily, then the glaze returned. "Aw, no. What is that, some kinda chewin' tobacco or somethin'?"

"Yeah. Or somethin'." I took a pinch of the moist stuff, feeling it burn pleasantly against my inner lip. It was all there: the roll of the boat, smell of the diesel exhaust, the good taste of Copenhagen—and a mission. I was back in Nam. I was ready to do what a very select group of us did better than any human beings in the history of the earth. Kill. Kill silently and professionally. Only this time I would enjoy it.

I winked at the kid when my dip was in place. I knew the black guy was just inside Billy's cabin listening to everything I said. And he probably had a gun trained on me.

"Look," I said, "I think what happened is, you hit those pilings and knocked your prop off. No big thing; I can have ya goin' again in five minutes— after I get my spare prop out of the hold, that is. You're welcome to use it; I trust you. But you'll have to help me. I'm by myself, and someone has to hold the hatch up."

The kid glanced nervously behind him as if looking for some signal that it was okay to board my boat. He turned to me. "Hey, that's great. Yeah, jes' put on a new propeller. Far out!"

Clumsily, he stepped over onto the *Sniper*, and when he rounded the cabin wall I was waiting. My knife was out, and I grabbed him by the throat, a firm deathgrip on the Adam's apple; the most effective come-along of all. The guy in the other boat couldn't see us now. I swung him down onto the deck, feeling his Adam's apple cartilaginous as a racketball within the confines of my big left hand. I placed the point of the Randall knife inside his ear, letting it cut just enough for him to know that it was there.

"Okay, asshole. Let's have a talk. And if you play innocent even once, I'll shove this knife through your ear and scramble your brains. The guys in the cigarette hull. Where'd they go? Where are they hiding out?"

I relaxed my grip on his throat. Just a little. The blond Blackbeard, the visionary drug runner, trembled beneath me. There were tears in his eyes. This was a real bummer. The biggest bummer of all. The day he would pay for his sins.

"Okay, okay, I'll tell ya, man. Only, don't kill me. *Please don't kill me.*"

I released my grip even more. I smiled. "Go ahead and talk, son."

"Up the Keys a ways. There's a private island. Offshore. Some big Senator or somethin' owns it. Day after tomorrow, we got a big pickup to make. Just needed an extra boat. I didn't want to kill that guy.

But up there, up there on Cuda Key, they told us to get a boat an' don't leave no witnesses. Had to do it, man. Had to do it."

I fought the overwhelming urge to shove the knife through his head. "Where's the rendezvous, son? Where are you going to make the pickup? When and where?"

"Right off Middle Sambo Key. Three a.m. Big load of cocaine."

"But when? What day?"

He sat up, rubbing his throat. I still had the knife ready. "Let me think, man. My mind—I been gettin' these blank spells lately. Let's see . . . yeah, Friday. Next Friday. Middle Sambo. That's it. Man, this drug business is some wild-ass trip, I'll tell ya."

He watched me as I put the knife back within the folds of shirt. The nervous smile had returned to the pallid face, and I knew what was on his mind. And I wanted him to do it. I wanted him to reach for that little stubnose. I wanted his hand to be on the cold grip of the pistol when I killed him. But before he made his move, I wanted him to hear something.

"That guy you killed. His name was Billy Mack. My best friend."

"Aw, Christ, I'm really sorry, man." Slowly, his hand moved toward his back pocket.

"He was one of the finest, bravest men I have ever known."

"Aw, shit. I can see why you were so bummed out."

I turned my head away, giving him every opportunity to make his move.

And he took it, jerking the pistol up awkwardly. But before he had a chance to fire, I chopped downward with the cutting edge of my right hand, breaking his wrist. The .38 spun away as if in slow motion. And almost in the same swoop of lethal hand, I chopped back across his neck, knocking his windpipe so awry, and with such force, that it looked as if he had swallowed half a small hula hoop.

He floundered on the deck of my boat like a tarpon taken too green, eyes bugging out, clawing at his ruined neck. I held him down against the deck with my foot, watching him die.

"Charlie! What in the hell's goin' on over there, Charlie?"

Carefully, I peeked through the salon windows. It was the black guy. The one who had killed Billy Mack, the man who had slit the throat of my best friend. And he was loaded for bear. In his hand he carried a big ugly .357 Auto Mag, a singularly merciless handgun. I studied my assault rifle, snug in its clips. It would have been so easy to sever that flat ugly head of his with one burst.

But that's not how I wanted to do it.

I knew how I wanted Billy Mack's murderer to die.

IV

Quickly and quietly, I removed my pants and slid off the stern of the *Sniper* into the clear turquoise sea. Below me, purple sea fans stood out black against the white sand depths. I didn't need a mask. In the SEALS I had become more fish than man.

I took a good deep bite of summer air, then noiselessly swam beneath my boat to the stern of Billy Mack's. As I had guessed, the prop was gone, the driveshaft bent.

I surfaced by the diver's deck, mounted at water level. I could still hear the guy yelling for the poor little dead blond pirate. Testing every movement, every motion, for noise, I pulled myself up onto Billy's boat and slid across the bleached teak deck on my belly.

I could see him plainly now. He was poised on the foredeck, leaning over the storm railing, trying to peer into the cabin where his friend has disappeared.

He held the .357 Auto Mag at ready. His back was to me: a huge guy, taller than I, almost as broad through the shoulders, and much heavier.

"Charlie! Goddam, Charlie, we gotta get our asses outta here!"

I wanted him to yell. Every time he opened his mouth, I was three feet closer.

"Mister man, you better let that boy outta there, hear? I'll come over there an' blow your white ass off with this here gun, I will!"

The tendency is to leap at someone you want to take from behind. That's the way the amateurs do it; the makers of gaudy western shoot-'em-ups. But I didn't leap. Too much chance of making a mistake, missing your target. And I had done it too many times before.

I could have whispered into his ear before I took him. But I didn't. I grabbed him around the neck with my left arm and, with my right, jabbed my knife a safe half inch into the soft underbelly of his chin.

"*Drop it, asshole!*"

Oh, he was strong. Awesome. But not awesome enough. The pistol exploded harmlessly. *Wham-wham-wham.*

"Do I not yet have your attention, *asshole*?"

I kneed him at the base of the spine and let the knife slide in half an inch farther. I knew that he could now feel the point beneath the base of his tongue.

"Drop it!"

He half-threw the .357 into the blue water. I pulled

the knife out of his chin and held it beneath his Adam's apple.

"You 'bout cut my goddam tongue out, cap'in!" He frothed black fresh blood as he spoke. "You ain't gonna kill me, are you, cap'in?"

"This boat we're standing on—you killed the guy who owned it, didn't you? Tell me the truth, asshole, or you're dead where you stand!"

"Yeah! But I didn't want ta. Had orders, cap'in. Told us ta go out an' get a boat, so that's wha' we did."

"Who's 'they'?"

"Men up ta Cuda Key, that's who. Never really met 'em. They just give orders, tells me what ta do, and I do it."

"The guy you killed was my best friend. His name was Billy Mack. And it was the biggest mistake of your life, asshole."

He half moaned, "Oh Jesus, cap'in. Shoot me if ya have to, but please don' cut my goddam throat out."

"That's what you did to Billy!"

"Just tryin' to make a livin', cap'in!"

I shoved the stench of him away from me. Sometimes I think Mark Twain was right. The human race is just too pathetic for words. He whirled back to face me, spitting blood. And I thought, what kind of animal is it who will murder for a few dollars? And then I realized: wasn't that what I was doing in Vietnam?

Okay, so I was a murderer, too. But there it was kill or be killed. And here, I would make sure it was the same; an indulgence of my own frail morality.

"All right, asshole, give it your best shot. Billy never had a chance. You do. Kill me or I'll cut your throat."

He was no longer the shuffling, humble Negro. He was black and fierce; huge nostrils flared; a trapped animal.

"Big mistake you just made, white boy. Big mistake!" I saw him look past my shoulder, as if there were someone behind me. But I would have none of that.

"Shoot 'em, Mr. Benjamin! Why'nt ya shoot 'em?" And still he looked behind me, black eyes widening as if in some terrible realization. It was the oldest trick in the world.

I was crouched and ready when he swung at me, the huge fist whooshing past my ear. And I caught the fist as if it were a fastball and squeezed it, feeling fingers crush beneath my grip, twisted the right arm around behind him, lifting him high off the foredeck of the boat, hearing the shoulder explode within the socket.

He shrieked with pain, face contorted with horror. And my Randall knife was already traveling on its flat, swift arc. It razored through his neck as if it were composed of cheese, snapping his head back in rhythmic convulsions of blood, spurt-spurt-spurting, mixing with the blood of Billy Mack, now dried black in the hot August sun. In his wide eyes, there was a dreadful expression of serenity. And I watched his lungs deflate and life evaporate, as if he were a lanced toy balloon.

Okay, Billy Mack. You died a very, very nasty death. But their deaths were nastier. They knew that it was coming. I saw the horror in their eyes.

And that's when I felt the cold muzzle of a .45-caliber service automatic being jammed into my back.

So the big black guy hadn't been using some simpleminded ploy. There had been someone behind me.

Three guys. Not two—as Nels had told me.

And I knew that I was dead.

He was good. He prodded me in the back with the weapon, then moved away to a safe distance. Such a little thing, but, as with any profession of skill—such as in the profession of war and killing—an expert can tell a lot from very, very little. This guy wouldn't be the pushover the other two had been.

"Would you mind very much, Captain MacMorgan, if I asked you to toss that handsome Randall knife of yours into the water? No, in front of you. Right off the bow. That's right. Seems a shame, doesn't it—to waste a knife of that quality. But I'm afraid it's necessary."

I tossed the knife ahead of me, watching it flutter, then tumble through the clear water. A big barracuda, seeing the flash of silver, was on it in an instant. But the barracuda stopped short when it realized it wasn't a fish; drifting backward, stiletto-shaped and menacing.

I had heard that voice before, but where? There was an odd silkiness to it; kind of voice you might expect to hear pounding away at you over the radio.

Buy our toilet tissue, or buy our dish soap, because it's the very, very best, new and improved, etc. etc. All words enunciated just right; the voice projected and deadly, deadly self-assured.

Where had I heard it before?

"If you will be so kind, Captain MacMorgan—no, *don't* turn around—let's move to the aft deck. That's right, walk backward, slow and easy. You see, I know what you are thinking right now. You're measuring distances, considering odds, wondering what the possibilities of surviving are if you dive into the water or, perhaps, even try to leap over onto your own boat. You see, *Dusky* MacMorgan, I've always been smarter than you. And better. Much better. Always."

And then I knew.

He backed me to the fighting deck, then had me lie belly-down, my feet to the stern rail, the forward hull of *Ernie's Honor* safely behind him.

I looked up then and saw the man I knew I would see; the man I had known for so short a time and hated so much, long, long ago in Vietnam.

Benjamin Ellsworth. *Lieutenant* Benjamin Ellsworth.

A college boy who loved weapons. ROTC ace, then lieutenant j.g. And, when the good officers started getting killed off in those first unpublicized years in Nam, he came to be our OIC. Oh, how he swaggered. And primped. And browbeat. Very military. Very superior. And very much a coward.

It didn't take us long to find out. All our group ever wanted was a mission—and we had plenty of them. Before he came. Afterward, none. Not one. He always found a way to slide us out of them. When men who are trained to fight have no enemy, they end up fighting themselves. And that's what happened with us. We got sloppy. We began to bitch and quarrel like spoiled children. Morale had never been worse. And still he swaggered, springing surprise inspections when we should have been carrying out surprise attacks.

So, one night I went to his hooch. Alone. He sat beneath the light of a Coleman lantern cleaning that ivory-handled .45 of his. He affected irritation at being interrupted by a lowly seaman—SEAL or not.

"What is it, MacMorgan?"

"May I speak plainly, sir?"

"If you can manage, MacMorgan."

So I told him. Told him everything. Told him about the bickering, the crumbling morale. And he was outraged.

"Are *you* attempting to tell *me* how to command? Why, you stupid boot, I spent four years in college learning my job." He glowered at me. "I know all about you, MacMorgan. Circus orphan. The tough guy everybody likes. Well, let me tell you something, swabbie—I *don't* like you. Not even a little bit. In fact, I think you're one of the most stupid human beings I've ever met!" He shuffled through some papers on his desk as if looking for my file. "My God, you didn't even graduate from high school—and *you're* trying to tell *me*? If that wasn't so absurd it would be funny!"

"May I still speak plainly, sir?"

"Yes!"

"The men think you're a coward, sir. And I agree. I think you're yellow."

He started to get up out of his chair, then thought better of it. He jammed a cartridge into his ivory-handled automatic.

"Get out of here, MacMorgan! I don't ever want to see that baby face of yours in my quarters again!"

"If Lieutenant Ellsworth would be willing to take his blouse off and step outside, perhaps we could settle this like men."

He had pointed the .45 at me then. "Get out of here, MacMorgan. I don't have anything to prove to trash like you. I'll be running this man's Navy when you're sweeping up bars for a living."

So this was the guy who stood above me now, probably that same .45 automatic pointed at my head. He hadn't lasted long in the Navy. Ass-kissing and brown-nosing will only take you so high. Not long after we finally got rid of him, we heard he had gotten mixed up in the black market somehow. They said he was getting rich. They said Lieutenant Ellsworth could get you anything, absolutely anything, you wanted. And even later, I heard that he had resigned his commission under hazy circumstances.

"Hah! I see you finally recognize me, MacMorgan!"

I looked up at him. The angular, ferret face had aged considerably. But the build was the same: just under six feet tall, lean and wiry, the way an English professor might look if he did a little weight lifting. Jet-black hair, thin girlish lips, hands that looked as if they were made to shuffle papers.

"Yeah, I recognize you, Ellsworth."

He sneered at me. "You know, it amuses me to think that I will be the one to kill you. I could have shot you when you suckered poor Charlie into your cabin. Or when, in typically and absurdly heroic style, you gave Big Bart a chance. I could have shot you so easily. I was right behind you, you know." He gave a weird little laugh. "But frankly, I wanted to see who was going to win. I was very impressed, the way you handled Bart. Almost proud, in a strange sort of way. Bart was a good man—not like Charlie. Charlie was pathetic. But, the same as in the Navy, you have to work with so many pathetic people in this business. So I was glad I didn't shoot you—then. I wanted to have a chance to have a little chat." He chuckled again. "You see, Seaman Mack— what was his first name again? Billy, yes. Well, Mr. Billy Mack didn't have much time for conversation. You always liked killing, didn't you, MacMorgan? Always gung-ho, ready for a fight? Well, you would have enjoyed seeing the way Big Bart killed your little friend. He flopped around on the deck like a fish. Blood just everywhere—that's *right*, MacMorgan, try to get up. *Try* to jump me. You're just stupid enough to try it."

"You're crazy, Ellsworth. You're crazy and you're a coward."

"Yeah, I'm crazy. Crazy like a fox. Crazy and rich.

I want you to tell me one last thing before I put a bullet through your brain. Did poor little Charlie tell you anything about our . . . our little operation when you had him down below?"

"He told me everything."

He had lifted his gun, ready to fire. He looked at me in shrewd appraisal. "I've always been much too smart for you, MacMorgan. Had poor Charlie told you anything at all, you would have lied. You would have said he told you nothing. But it doesn't matter, MacMorgan. You're about to pay for calling me yellow back in Vietnam—"

"*Hold it!*"

It was the woman. Mrs. Johnson. She stood on the port walkway of Billy Mack's boat, my Russian AK-47 in her hands, pointing it awkwardly at Lieutenant Benjamin Ellsworth. She did look fine: denim shirt flapping slightly in the light August breeze, breasts full and firm beneath, blond hair looking gold in the sunlight. Ah, she was a brave one. A good one. I could imagine her teddy-bear husband whimpering down below. And I thought: If I'm going to die, it's at least nice to go with someone as brave as her in my mind; someone to replace the awful, bottomless insanity of Ellsworth.

Because I was going to die. And so was she. And so was her husband.

At a glance, Ellsworth saw what I saw. He laughed loudly. "Mrs. MacMorgan, it's nice of you to try to save your husband—but you've forgotten one thing. You've forgotten to arm your weapon."

It was true. That ugly crescent cartridge clip was missing.

The lovely face fell, horrified. She looked to me for confirmation. I nodded. And mustered up a brave wink; a wink because I wanted her to go out with at least a little hope, and because I was so, so sorry that blind bad luck had caused them to charter the boat of Billy Mack's best friend, this one awful August day.

"Come on down and join us, Mrs. MacMorgan. I'd like to get a closer look at the woman stupid enough to marry this droll human being who lies before me."

"She's not my wife, Ellsworth! Let her go. She doesn't know a damn thing."

"Sure, sure, MacMorgan. I'm surprised you found such a pretty lady, frankly."

The woman stood beside him now, shrunken, slack, as if she were in shock.

"But you know, it's hard to see how pretty you are with all those clothes on."

"Don't!"

He leveled the gun at me again. "Don't move again, MacMorgan. Don't lift a finger, or you'll watch her die."

Her lips were trembling, her entire body shaking. Ellsworth reached up with his left hand, still watching me, and ripped her shirt open. Buttons skittered over the teak deck. She was braless beneath the shirt; brown cones of breast pointed skyward.

"Lisa-lee! Lisa-lee, what's going on out there?"

Lisa-lee—so that was her first name.

Ellsworth raised his eyebrows. "Ah, so we're about to have another guest, huh?"

Her husband peeked around the cabin wall, then ducked back in, like a turtle.

Ellsworth smiled. "Well, maybe this will bring our frightened friend out. Get down on your knees, woman!"

As she dropped to her knees, facing Ellsworth, he pulled the shirt off her. Her skin glistened in the sun. I knew what he wanted her to do. And I hated the thought of it. Slowly, his eyes darting from me to her, from her back to me, he unzipped his pants. And that's when I decided. I decided I would force him to shoot. It didn't matter. He would kill me anyway. And just as I was about to leap at him, hoping I would at least get my hands on his throat before he shot me down, Lisa-lee Johnson, that pallid, terrified woman, reached back and gave him such a fist to the groin that had it been his heart it would have killed him.

It didn't kill him, of course. But he howled. And, with me already in motion, I was on him before he even had time to shoot. Like a linebacker nailing a little tailback, I hit him with such force that his neck jerked back with a loud *pop* and the gun flew out of his hand into the water. I hoped I hadn't killed him. I wanted to hurt him, to punish him. I wanted him to live—for a while.

He wasn't dead. He started up at me, and when he did I kicked him full in the face. He lay there choking on his own teeth, and then he turned an awful face toward us. "They'll get you for this, MacMorgan. You'll pay for this, you silly naive bastard!"

Lisa-lee Johnson held close to me, trembling, feeling very small.

"Lisa-lee, go back to my boat. Back to the cabin. Get some clothes on."

"You're not going to kill him!"

"What?"

She sagged against me, her arms holding me. She was crying, tears dripping down onto her bare breasts. "I can't take any more, Dusky. I can't listen to another scream. Please, oh please, Dusky, let the police have him. He'll be imprisoned. Or go to the electric chair. *Please!*"

Gently, I pushed her away from me. I was the madman, now. Oh, I was going to kill him, all right. Lieutenant Benjamin Ellsworth was about to die with the hands of a trashy high-school-dropout circus orphan at his throat. Oh yes, I would kill him. And make it last as long as I could.

I jerked him to his feet, slapping him to make sure he was conscious. And just when I got my hands around his throat, just as his eyes started to bug, that's when the Coast Guard jet helicopter came roaring over. They were screaming at me over the PA system. And Lisa-lee, with her tiny hands, was trying to pry my huge ones away from the throat of Ellsworth.

"They'll try *you* for murder, Dusky. Think of your wife, for God's sake. They'll arrest *you!*"

So the Coast Guard carted Lieutenant Benjamin Ellsworth away, his bloody face smirking, his promise still ringing in my ears: "They'll get you for this. You'll pay. . . ."

But they would arrest him for murder. And try him. And send him to prison. Or the electric chair. Because this is the United States of America. Home of the brave, land of the free. Where judges are fearless in their application of the law. Where lawyers are servants of the public, battling for what is right. Where justice is blind, blind, blind.

Sure it is.

Absolutely.

No doubt about it.

Right. . . .

V

It took exactly five days for Ellsworth's threats to become a reality. Five days, seven hours, and thirty-some minutes. I know because I looked at my Rolex when I heard the explosion. And when I realized that the sound of the explosion came from the direction of our home on Elizabeth Street, the time was seared into my memory for the hellish eternity I knew my life would be from that moment on.

Ellsworth was right. Correct on every point. I was naive. And stupid. And "they" would get even.

They didn't kill me. But they tried. And, in trying, they did what I had done to Charlie, the pill-eyed blond pirate. They tore my life away at the throat. I wasn't dead, but I was a corpse. A living, walking corpse.

When I finally got back to the docks with the Johnsons, I had resigned myself to the fact that it all wasn't just a bad dream, a blue-water vision that occasionally befalls the solitary open-ocean sailor: dreams that can either horrify or delight, but always seem very, very real indeed right down to the last detail. No, the look on Lisa-lee Johnson's face alone was testament enough to the reality of it all. She had retreated to a far corner of the *Sniper*, alone, shrunken, looking very pale, while her beefy husband pouted below. He was outraged that she could have allowed that vile man with the pistol to rip her shirt off. The nerve of that woman! Traipsing around bare-chested in front of total strangers!

He was shocked and outraged by the whole episode. No burst of realization in that chubby husband: *That is one magnificent human being I have as a wife.* Her bravery was wasted on him.

As they filed off my boat, staggered by the violence which occurs daily in this world, but had only been bad half-hour TV dramas in their world, I tried to apologize to Lisa-lee.

"Mrs. Johnson, had I known . . . had I had any idea . . ."

She looked up at me, her blue eyes troubled, her brain scanning to make some sense of it all.

I said, "Don't try to reason it out. There are some very bad things in this world. Very bad. Today, you got a little glimpse of them. But don't try to make them fit into some orderly scheme, some great and glowing plan, because they won't. I know. I've tried."

She smiled, then, a narrow, sharp smile—the kind you might have expected to see on the face of Mark Twain. "Crazy world, huh?"

"Yeah."

"My husband didn't catch his world-record fish."

"His wrist . . . I really am sorry about that. I expect to pay all the doctor—"

She held her hand up. "We're insured for everything. We should be. He sells it. Insured clear up until the time he takes his last passive breath."

"Don't be too hard on him."

She reached up and touched my face; touched it as she had on the boat before it had all happened. "I'm the better for you, Captain Dusky MacMorgan. And I won't be too hard on him—in fact, I'll be quite the opposite. And I'll mail your shirt back to you the first chance I get."

She turned to walk away, then stopped, hesitated, looked back at me. "He really would have killed us, huh?"

"Yes," I said. "Yes, he would have killed us all."

She nodded, thinking, then turned and followed her outraged husband back into her own life.

Timing is an odd thing. Take a side street instead of the main street and you miss the drunken driver who, on a different day, would run the stop sign and bring your innocent existence to a fiery end. You leave the house thirty seconds too early on a nondescript day for a pack of gum at the corner store, and you miss the telephone call which would have altered the course of your whole life. As I tied up my *Sniper* I wondered what might have happened had Billy Mack decided not to go after dolphin that day; wondered what if he had made it back to the docks.

Wondered what if Mr. Johnson had taken his world-record Atlantic; what if, to celebrate, he had taken me and Billy and Lisa-lee down to Sloppy Joe's; what if Billy and Lisa-lee had hit it off, as I knew they would have. What if, indeed. . . .

But Billy wasn't coming back to the docks that day or any day. His *Ernie's Honor* would be towed back in later, quiet as a coffin, and we would never crack a beer after a day's fishing and shoot the breeze again.

No, the only person to meet me on the docks that day, as I drained down a cold Hatuey, trying to figure out how I was going to break the news about Billy to Janet and the boys, was a tiny, official-looking man in a gray suit. He strode up as if he were seven feet tall, filled with his own importance. He stopped at my slip, flashed a badge in my face, then started to step aboard.

"Hold it, partner." He stopped. "How 'bout asking permission before you step onto my vessel?"

He looked slightly flustered. "Mr. MacMorgan, my name is Lenze. Arnold Lenze, and I'm with the federal government. I head up a special task force mandated to investigate drug smuggling and drug-smuggling-related crimes, and then to prosecute. We work with the blessing of local law-enforcement agencies, but independently of them and beyond their authority. I want a statement from you."

"Fine," I said. "Ask to come aboard, and I'll talk your ear off."

He flushed, more than just a tad pissed off. Federal government. One of the superior few. Well, I knew his type. One of the thousands of people who couldn't make it in the free-enterprise system, so made a blind reach for solvency and came up with the government teat. Leach of the bureaucracy; leach of the people. They suck us dry with their self-importance and their federal programs.

"Mr. Lenze," I said, "I'm not trying to give you a hard time. I'm really not. But this has been one of the nastier days, and I don't think a little common courtesy is too much to ask."

"MacMorgan, you're very damn lucky I don't arrest you and charge you with attempted murder!"

"What?"

"That's right! Mr. Ellsworth gave me a very interesting statement."

"Ellsworth was with the two druggies. He's part of the operation—"

"He told his story, and he also told us what you would say. MacMorgan, Mr. Ellsworth is a highly respected civil servant in Miami—"

"*What did he say?*"

"He told us the truth, I assume. That he was kidnapped to be used as a hostage by those two men that he killed."

"That he killed!"

"That's right. That he struggled free of the ropes with which he was tied after being loaded into the stolen boat, that he overpowered his two captors, and then you came along. He said that you had recognized your friend's boat, and that you were ready to kill somebody, anybody, and that you especially wanted to kill him because he was your superior in the Navy. Frankly, I can relate to that because I myself was a lieutenant in the Army, and my men often threatened to kill me."

"Lenze, he fed you bullshit. Raw bullshit! My God, there are witnesses. Two of them just left!"

He pushed his glasses up off the bridge of his nose and opened a manila folder. "Good. Give me their names and their addresses, and we'll get in touch with them."

"Johnson," I said. "But I don't know their address. From someplace in New York, I think."

He looked up at me. "You have no address? Mr. MacMorgan, there are probably a hundred thousand Johnsons in New York. I need something a little more specific. What motel are they staying in?"

"They left for home today—wait a minute, you can catch them at the hospital if you hurry. Mr. Johnson had a broken wrist."

"Did one of the two boat thieves do it?"

"No, I did—and there were three, not two. Ellsworth was—"

"MacMorgan, I've already taken a statement from one Nels Chester. He told me four men—two black, two white—were involved in the theft. He said that a black man and a white man killed Mr. William Mack, and then made off with his boat. Mr. Ellsworth says he killed the two men—"

"I did!"

"—one black, one white. It gives countenance to his story. Tell me, MacMorgan, why did you break Mr. Johnson's wrist?"

I closed my eyes, shaking my head. I couldn't believe it.

"MacMorgan, before I came here I had a phone call from a United States Senator. A very important Northern Senator who vacations in Florida and knows Mr. Ellsworth very well. He told me Mr. Ellsworth was one of the finest, most honest men he knew. And I believe that, MacMorgan. So why don't you just tell me the truth? Mr. Ellsworth isn't going to press charges—that's the kind of man he is, apparently. He says he understands your grief at the loss of your friend. Frankly, if you had tried it on me, buster, I'd have seen your tail in prison."

"Get out of here, Lenze."

"What?"

"Get the hell out of my sight."

"MacMorgan, I came here to get a statement, and I'm going to get it. If that means arresting you, I'll do it."

So I gave him a statement, complete with information about the planned cocaine pickup off Middle Sambo Reef. And he wrote and poked at his glasses, looking at me with contempt all the while. And as we talked, I knew that Lisa-lee Johnson and her husband were motoring north, taking any hopes of seeing Benjamin Ellsworth behind bars with them.

* * *

They cleared Ellsworth and released him on Tuesday, on the same day we buried Billy Mack; the same day my world exploded.

I got the word from a friend of mine at the Key West sheriff's department; a good man, Rigaberto Herrera. Inspector Rigaberto Herrera. One of the hundreds of thousands of Cubans who came to the United States when Castro and Khrushchev took control of that island paradise ninety miles to the south. One of the many who refused to become a part of the welfare roll; one of the many who were too proud to allow their poverty to reduce them to drinking wine and dancing island dances in a ghetto. He had lost his homeland but, like so many other Cubanos, he hadn't lost his dignity. He went to work. And he worked hard. He learned the language. He powered his way to a bachelor's degree in criminology in three highly concentrated years, going to class and studying days, working at a restaurant nights. He not only didn't seek government aid, he refused it. No bitching about the tough life that was his, no moaning that the soft brown color of his skin made it impossible for him to succeed without financial assistance. He moved up quick in the sheriff's department. And he was still moving.

He approached me just before Billy's funeral, giving me a quick embrace.

"I'm sorry about your friend, *amigo*. I know how close you two were."

"He would have wanted you to come, Rigaberto. I'm glad to see you."

We stood in the icy air conditioning of the funeral-home lobby. The sickly-sweet smell of refrigerated flowers was everywhere. Organ music played in the next room. What an absurd custom, funerals. How I wished, then, that I had had the nerve to steal poor Billy away, wrap him in nice white canvas, weight him down, and roll him over somewhere in the Gulf Stream. He would have liked that. He would have liked it a lot more than the somber pomp of the great American sendoff; expensive platitudes and bullshit coffin niceties that only add more pain to the already painful human condition.

"I need to speak with you a moment, Dusky. Alone."

"Now?"

"Yes. Maybe we could take a little walk. We've got a few minutes before the services start."

I peeked into the next room. Janet, in her darkest dress, and little blond Ernest and Honor sat on the folding chairs before the closed casket, not crying, not looking, just lost and filled with soft horror. I felt so, so sorry for them all.

"Sure," I said. "But let's make it quick."

We walked to the corner, turning north on Duval Street. The panhandlers and street freaks were already on the move, filling old Key West and the warm August morning with a strange sense of desperation.

"So what's up?"

Rigaberto hesitated—unusual, for he is one of the toughest, most straightforward people I know.

He toyed with his black mustache nervously.

"I'm not sure how to start," he said. "I'm not even sure what or how much to tell you."

"What the hell is it, Rigaberto?"

He stopped and turned toward me. Behind him there was a wide gray-and-green banyan tree, air shoots hanging down like bars. "There's something strange going on, Dusky. Something odd about the whole short investigation into that Ellsworth character."

"You heard my side of the story?"

He nodded. "Yeah. And I believe you—and not just because you're a good friend. My cop sense tells me it's true. But Lenze and the rest of those federal characters had their investigation over and him out of town so fast that it made my head spin."

"So they did release him?"

"Yeah. It was the same way the CIA boys used to operate when one of their people got messed up in something local. Wham-bang, thank you ma'am. Everything nice and neat, no loose ends."

"Do the other people down at your office smell something sour?"

"*Yo lo creo!*" He smiled. "Sorry about the Spanish—when I get excited, or really pissed off, my heritage takes over."

"So what are you now?"

"Pissed off. My boss wants to get permission to start an investigation of our own. The trouble there is you don't know how high you have to go before you know it's safe to ask. Where does the stink end?

With Lenze? I doubt it. There are some big boys behind this one. We don't go high enough, ask the
wrong one, and that's the end of it. Permission
denied."

"Lenze said he couldn't find my eyewitnesses,
the Johnsons."

Rigaberto chuckled derisively. "It would have
taken me—or any other competent cop—probably
just a day. It all stinks, Dusky. The whole business
stinks."

"What about the cocaine pickup Friday? Are you
going to have some people out there?"

"We've been told hands off. Strictly a federal project. They say we're letting too great a percentage of
the drugs get past us. And God knows it's true. But
with our limited staff, with the amount of drug running going on—well, maybe we do need help. I don't
know. But not that kind of help." He shrugged. "I
just wanted you to know we weren't just going to
let it drop. You've got some supporters. You believe me?"

I put my hand on his shoulder. Rigaberto Herrera:
five-eight, five-nine, maybe; 160 pounds, dripping
wet. But as tough and as smart as they come. "I
believe you, *amigo*." We turned and walked back
toward the funeral home. "How's the wife and
kids?"

"Rigaberto Jr. hit two home runs night before last
against Fort Myers. They say he has a shot at the
pros."

When we got to the funeral home, he took my arm,

stopping me. "Look, Dusky, I'm going to tell you something you probably already know. They might be after you, now. You killed two of their boys, and they don't let that sort of shit go unpunished."

"I can take care of myself, inspector."

I saw a little flash of anger flare in his dark eyes. "Oh, sure *you* can. It would take four guys with automatics, and you'd have to be unarmed, and they'd still have to be damn lucky—I know all that crap, MacMorgan. But what about *them*?" He motioned toward the funeral home. "What about Janet and the kids?"

"I can take care of them, too."

"Bullshit!" His eyes softened. "Listen, we're friends, Dusky. You helped me when the rest of the gringos looked upon us Cubans as just more darkies asking for the welfare dole. Now I'm trying to help you. Let me. I'm going to assign a man to keep an eye on your house. Nothing obvious. Starting tomorrow, say. Keep him on it for a couple of weeks. No harm in that, is there?"

I sighed, smiled. "Okay, Rigaberto. You're right and I'm wrong. Send your man. I appreciate it. I really do, *amigo*."

So we put Billy Mack into the ground; buried him in the old Key West cemetery shoulder to shoulder with three hundred years of oceangoing, boat-building, rum-running, gun-running, gamefishing Key Westers. Not really *in* the ground. Atop the ground; cemented into a crypt, above the limestone base which is the accumulative skeleton of a million years of sea creatures. Life stacked upon life, death stacked upon death. How we do go around and around.

When the services were over, Janet had the good sense to leave me alone there in the cemetery. She reached up, hugged me, tears in her blue eyes.

"Walk home, if you like," she had said. "Stop down by the docks, take your boat out, have a couple of beers. You'll feel better, hon."

"Thanks, Jan."

"You want me to keep dinner hot?"

"Naw. Be home about dark, probably."

Ernest and Honor clung close to my legs, both already thigh-high, blond hair as fine as spun glass. They seemed sobered by the dark atmosphere of the cemetery.

Honor, the introspective one, surveyed the rows of tombs like a wizened old philosopher. "We're all gonna be here someday, aren't we, Daddy?"

"Maybe, Honnie, maybe."

Ernest reddened, tears starting to stream down his face for the first time all day. "I'm gonna get those guys, Daddy! Those guys that killed Uncle Billy— I'm gonna beat them all up! I'm gonna . . . gonna kick their *asses*!"

I swept him up and held him close. "Now, now, Ernie, Uncle Billy wouldn't like you cussing like that."

"Well, I am!"

Funny, brave little man. Janet and I often kidded that the hospital had somehow gotten their names reversed. Honor would be the observer, the artist; Ernest would be the knightly one, the guy you could knock down and knock down, but who would still keep on battling.

As Janet and the boys started to leave, I heard myself call her name. She turned around, surprised as I.

"What, Dusky?"

"I . . . I . . . guess I just wanted to say that I love you, Janet. Love you more than anything. Always."

She looked at me with the fondness only people who really love each other know.

"And you're the best thing that ever happened to me, Dusky. Ever."

So they left me there with the remains of my best friend.

"I got them, Billy Mack. I killed two of them. But it didn't bring you back, goddammit. Nothing will ever bring you back."

So what do you do?

Walk the August streets with hands in pockets, whistle an aimless tune. Smile at the little Key West children, nod politely at the dying elderly, knowing that each and every one of us is being sucked down by the whirl of life, being flushed toward the vacuum. Buy a *Herald* to see what's up with the rest of the world.

Dark thoughts on a bright tropical day.

Iranians on the rampage, Haitians fleeing, dark-skinned people angry at the white-skinned; drunken driver kills four more innocent, no more gas, and the price of gold is going crazy. I watched a big herring gull soar above Old Town, bank toward the sun, and burst into white flame. The little things stick with you, the beautiful little things. Golden gulls and pretty children and polite old people. The screams of the newspapers disappear forever when you wrap the fish and take out the garbage.

Walk toward the docks, through the little park. Kids on playground equipment, new mothers with fresh faces and fresh hopes. Wink a secret wink at a stray dog and show off for the kids.

"See how that big man swung on the bar, Mommy? Did you see him swing up and do the double backflip? How'd he do that, Mommy? Huh?"

Once I got to the *Sniper*, I cracked a cold Hatuey and drank it with some haste. And then I opened another, sipping at it while I oiled reels, made new leaders, spliced fresh line to old. Sweat began to roll off my nose, the hot sun feeling good. I finished the beer, went below, and changed into a pair of khaki shorts. Few things feel as good on a hot day as changing from funeral suit to shorts. So, for lack of anything else to do, I fired up the twin GMCs, feeling the good muffled rumble move through my body, and headed *Sniper* out Key West Bight, picked up Marker 29, and ran her full-bore out Man of War Harbor, wind in my face on the fly bridge, green roll of sea beneath.

Progressively, I felt better. We all die. And life goes on. Always. No matter what.

Back in Key West, I treated myself to black beans,

yellow rice, and the best fried yellowtail on earth at
El Cacique. I overtipped the pretty young waitress,
Alicia, and she winked a pretty dark eye, knowing
that flirting with me was safe, that I had a wife I
loved back home. So I walked a Crystal beer down
to the docks. It was nearly sunset, and the street
freaks and drugheads were there, watching that great
orange ball melt into the turquoise distance. Conga
drums and the cry of the conch-salad man, smell of
open sea and frangipani and jasmine; exotic Key
West. I wondered what Papa would have thought
about all the changes on the island, and I remembered the last time I had seen him. It was my final
winter with the circus, the winter before that August
when the only family I had ever known was murdered. He sought me out that last time. He was about
to leave for Cuba. It was March. He saw that our
circus was in town. He stopped by to say hello, and
asked me to arrange a meeting with our lion tamer.
I did; he was delighted. He loved the big cats. I
walked him to the cages; that big gray-bearded man
now looking older and sadder than I could ever remember. He watched a big male tiger we had called
Captain; watched him pace his nervous figure eights
within the confines of that narrow cage. He watched
for a long time, his breath coming soft and shallow,
and then he turned to me.

"Right there, old-timer—that's how I feel.
Trapped."

"How trapped, Papa?"

He smacked himself on the ·chest. "In here. I'm

trapped inside this old carcass of mine. Things starting to go bad. Eyes giving out—and I used to have
fine eyes. Almost as fine as my father's. Legs going,
heart going. And I feel trapped in here, too." He
tapped himself on the forehead. "Nothing worse than
that sort of trapped."

Slowly, Papa stuck his hand inside the cage to the
big cat. It struck me that I should have jerked him
away—but I could never have done that. Not to him.
The indignity would have been worse than losing a
hand. The cat stopped, yellow eyes glowing, sniffed the
hand, and then moved away, strangely uninterested.

Papa laughed. "He knows, old-timer. Only people
like him and me—and you; you, too—will ever truly
appreciate the horror of that kind of trapped."

He seemed strange that night; distant. Before we
parted, he downed his seventh or eighth beer, looked
steadily at me, his eyes seeming to glow as the cat's
eyes had glowed.

"I want you to do some things for me, old-timer."

"Sure!" I was on about my fourth beer and feeling
fine. I would have done anything for him.

"First of all, I want you to stay out of the writing
business. Damn rough stuff. Does things to you."

"No problem there."

"And I want you to think about becoming a
fighter. You'd be one of the greatest of this century—
and I've seen 'em all. You're like a big cat on that
trap—too fast and too strong to be believed. And
what are you? Seventeen, eighteen?"

"Almost twenty," I lied. I wasn't quite sixteen yet.

He chuckled. "Sure, old-timer, sure. And I want you to do one other thing, okay?"

"Name it."

"If you can, come back to Key West. Take care of it. Too many jerks here now since they built that highway. This place is going to need some taking care of."

I had looked out across the black water, beyond Kingfish Shoals, toward the Tortugas. "I will, Papa. I mean it. I really will."

Two or three years later I read that Papa had finally escaped; left his disintegrating cage in his own private way.

So that's what I was thinking about when I heard the explosion. A sharp *crack* and rumble that made the island vibrate. The dopeheads loved it.

Far out!

It's the Japs, man, the Japs.

Almost eight-thirty p.m. by my Rolex. There was an odd roaring in my ears. And then I was running; running with a strange alien sob escaping from my lips. Because I knew. I knew without knowing. I ran for my life; the life they had just extinguished.

Sirens. Pulsing blue lights. I saw the remains of our old Chevy; blue splinters and twisted metal. And then Rigaberto was in front of me, trying to hold me back. He was crying; bawling like a child. And then everyone was trying to hold me back. But I had to save them. Had to help them. I was the invincible one, the unbeatable one, and only I could bring them back.

I broke through. And then wished I hadn't.

"They're gone, Dusky . . . Janet, the boys, gone . . ." It was Rigaberto, crying, still trying to turn me away.

"No . . ."

"I had a hunch . . . was going to watch myself tonight . . . too late, too goddam late . . . waved goodbye at me before she started the car. . . ."

"No. . . ."

A flower-scented evening in the tropics, and I stared on as if from above; as if soaring among the cold, cold stars and the dark chaos of mindless universe: my loves lay scattered like broken toys. . . .

VI

The cocaine boat lay anchored off Middle Sambo Reef, ghostly in the pale August moonlight. I waited for the pickup vessel to arrive, and watched, too, for any form of law-enforcement surveillance.

There was none.

I had left Key West at midnight in the stocky little Boston Whaler: just over thirteen feet of rugged, take-any-sea boat, powered with a fifty-horsepower Johnson. In a pinch, she'd do forty. I had powered five miles across the slow roll of frosted night sea, then broke out the oars and rowed the remaining mile to the lee side of the reef. The cocaine boat arrived about an hour later, noiselessly, showing no running lights. I breathed in the fresh night air; the sweet south wind blowing across from Cuba. Finally, something seemed real. After three blurry, hellish days of gauzy disbelief, nauseating guilt, and, finally, awful, awful realization, this, at least, seemed real.

I had gone through the funeral like a zombie. I spoke to no one, answered no one, refused to acknowledge condolences.

Former film star murdered!

It brought the newspaper ghouls on the run.

One beefy reporter approached after the funeral. Very demanding, very pushy. He said he'd been one of Janet's best friends before she "left the business." I owed him a statement. Some good quotes. Was I mixed up in drug running? How was she involved? Had she been hooked on something?

He watched me, a perplexed look on his face, when I started to smile. I reached into my pants pockets. It wasn't there. I finally located the little tin of snuff in my coat. There were a lot of people around. Curiosity seekers. The pretty actress and her two little boys had been blown to bits. My, my, what a shame. Any celebrities around that might give an autograph? What about that big blond guy—hadn't he starred with her in a film? No, that was the husband; the guy who had ruined her career and, finally, her life. The beefy newspaper reporter watched me slip the Copenhagen into my cheek.

"What the hell's the matter? Why're ya smiling like that? Listen, I realize this is a tough time for you, buddy, but I need a story. Came all the way down here from New York—"

I nailed him with an amber stinger—full in the right eye. He dropped his little notebook, howling.

"Goddam it, you can't treat the working press like that! You'll be hearing from our—"

He tried to sucker-punch me. Soft chubby round-house in slow motion. I brushed it away and stuck him good with a left. His nose collapsed, blood spattering the other reporters.

And then Rigaberto was there, guiding me away.

"Any of you other vultures want a story?"

"Don't bother with them, Dusky—they aren't worth the trouble."

"How about you, fat boy? UPI? I'll be glad to give you a story, too."

The reporters scattered in the face of this madness. I called them names. Childish obscenities you might hear from teenage boys readying for a fight none of them wanted. Only, I wanted to fight. Fight them all. I was ready to kill, and someone was going to die—them, me, it didn't matter.

"This is Dr. Robinson, Dusky. He's going to give you something to calm you down."

Muscular, good-looking man in a suit. There was a needle in his hand.

"How'd you like me to stick that hypo up your ass, sawbones?"

I never got a chance to hear his answer. Something stung my arm, and then, mercifully, there was nothing. . . .

Oh, the killers had done a professional job, all right. Rigaberto filled me in, sitting in a chair beside my hospital bed. Someone had sent flowers. Red roses. I didn't even bother to read the card. Outside, in the sterile hallways, nurses in white uniforms hurried back and forth while doctors so-and-so were paged softly over the telecom system.

"Before I tell you anything, Dusky, I want you to promise me something. This is a job for professional law enforcement, and I want you to promise you'll stay out of it. Okay?"

"Absolutely, *amigo*. Absolutely."

He knew I was lying. "I mean it, Dusky. This has all been tragic enough. I don't want to end up having to arrest you."

"Write out an oath and I'll sign it in blood."

He reached over and patted me on the forearm. "Dusky, there are just some things one man can't fight alone. Some things are just too big. This is one of those things. We're after them, Dusky; after them this very moment. And we'll get them—I promise you that."

"The way you got Ellsworth?"

"Goddammit, that's not fair, Dusky."

I knew it wasn't fair. But I didn't care. So I promised everything Rigaberto wanted me to promise. I didn't plan on honoring any of the promises, but Herrera was a good friend. Why put him on the spot by telling the truth?

"We figure they got hold of someone who knew your personal habits. Not hard to do on an island as small as this. But they don't figure on Billy Mack's funeral screwing up your routine. Normally, every evening, about eight-thirty or nine p.m., you hop in the car and drive down to the docks to check on your boat. So they planted a little ignition bomb. Nothing fancy—but just the right amount of explosives and in just the right spot. Professional. Very professional."

"So I try to avenge the murder of my best friend, and end up getting my wife and kids killed. God. . . ."

"Dusky! It wasn't your fault, dammit! Mourn for Janet, mourn for Ernie and Honor, but don't mourn for yourself. Don't let yourself go to ruin, Dusky. You owe them better than that."

That was true. I owed them better. Right then and there I decided to preserve myself, my strength, my sanity, and give them better. How many other Janets and Ernies and Honors had been left in the ruthless wake of those drug-running bastards? How many more would there be? The ones they didn't blow up would just end up among the walking dead: glazed eyes, vague smiles, hated pasts, and hopeless futures.

I would give them better. I would give them all better.

So I checked myself out on Friday morning. A hot Key West morning; the kind where the odor of asphalt shimmers up off the streets and the white clapboard houses and blue sea catch the sunlight and glow with oppressive, sleepy heat. Not a breeze, not a bird stirring. There was only the desperate whine of overworked air conditioners, vacationing cars on the molten streets, trapped smells of rotting fruit; mangos and limes and bananas.

Come to the happy tropics, historic Key West. Drink at Sloppy Joe's, walk past the Audubon house.

And watch your life dissolve while your brain cures like a Virginia ham.

Upon my request, Rigaberto had moved my clothes and a few other personal effects onto my boat. I would never go into that pretty little house on Elizabeth Street again. It was just another corpse, and I had had a stomach full of corpses. I climbed onto the *Sniper* feeling, as I did, a soft rush of nostalgia. I felt as if I hadn't been aboard in a year. I opened the cabin door, pushed open the forward windows, and stripped off my sodden clothes. I loved that boat. And love for a boat does not come with looking at blueprints in a boatyard, or with delivery day. It comes gradually, slowly, after years of working heavy seas, rainy nights underway, of fighting big fish and bigger blue northers, and always coming out on top, together. The *Sniper* was Janet's wedding present to me. She had her built up in Port Canaveral, with design help from Billy Mack and a naval-architect friend of ours from Sanibel Island. She was all the boat I could ever want. LOA: thirty-four feet, six inches. Thirteen-foot beam. Plenty of headroom in the salon, and 140 square feet of cockpit. She had an enormous fuel capacity that gave me a range of four hundred miles, with a safety factor of about fifty miles. She felt good, she smelled good. I got a cold beer from the little refrigerator, and turned the VHF to the AM band, and Radio Havana came blasting in. Bright conga music: steel drums and guitar. I washed the sweat away with a quick shower, and was already sweating again before I slipped into soft cotton shorts, knit shirt, and leather sandals.

This was my home now.

The *Sniper*.

Appropriate.

She had been equipped for hunting down and taking the big ones; the blue-water rogues that stalk the Gulf Stream. Si-Tex/Koden 707 digital readout loran C. Benmar autopilot. Furuno FE-502 white-line commercial fish finder. The best outriggers, the best rods and reels and line; the best of everything because that's what I, as a professional, demanded. Now I needed to outfit her for a different quarry. A bigger, smarter, and far less noble kind of game.

I sat at the little table in the salon and made a list.

D. Harold Westervelt was a friend of mine. One of my stranger friends. We had both survived military life and war, commando raids and espionage missions, but where I had married and found a new life, D. Harold could never leave the conflict behind. He loved it all too well. He lived in an ironically peaceful setting: suburban house near the naval base on Boca Chica Key. When he got too old for midnight assaults, the state department kept him on as sort of a freelance inventor. When it came to killing, Westervelt was indeed ingenious. They financed his sometimes strange notions and, in return, he produced for them highly sophisticated—albeit unusual—weaponry.

Those of us who held D. Harold's friendship—and there weren't many—and those of us who knew how

he made his living—even fewer still—often referred
to him as the Edison of Death.

It not only fit. It was accurate.

He was eating lunch when I arrived. Tossed salad
and unsweetened tea. A man of severe discipline, he
looked much younger than his fifty-odd years.
Shaved head, icy blue eyes, the lean steely look of an
Olympic 170-pound-class wrestler. He was dressed in
a white golfing shirt, blue serge pants with razor
creases, and well-oiled topsider shoes. He looked like
a retired German executive who had come to the
Keys to enjoy bridge and lawn sports.

"I was expecting you, captain." He got up from
the table, poured me a glass of iced tea, added the
teaspoon of honey. I had been to his home maybe
twice in eight years, and still he remembered how I
took it. We sat across from each other.

"It goes without saying that I was very sorry to
hear about your wife and children."

"How did you know I was coming? I didn't call."

He shrugged. "I know you, captain. Why belabor
the obvious?"

"Then maybe you know *why* I came?"

He stood, removed his dishes from the table,
washed them carefully in the sink, and stacked them
neatly to dry.

"Come with me."

I followed him through the kitchen, past the Jello-
blue swimming pool on the patio, down the hallway
to a padlocked fire door. He unlocked it and swung
it open, revealing his workshop. Except for one wall

lined with a marble workbench, there were locked gun cabinets everywhere. Every kind of handgun and military rifle. There were mementos of the Second World War, his many decorations framed and pinned to blue velvet; and American and British, Nazi and Russian uniforms on racks.

"We're similar end products from two different wars, captain. There's an interesting story behind the Nazi combat helmet with the bullet hole in it—but I won't bore you with my recollections. That's what happens to most old soldiers, you know. Like the warriors of all time, we become very, very boring." He studied me for a moment. "What have you gained? Ten, twelve pounds?"

"About seven."

"Hmm . . . I would have thought more. You'll need to lose the excess. At your age—thirty-five?—it can make a great deal of difference. Still using the snuff, I see. The stain on your index finger tells me so. Good. You never did use cigarettes—such a childish habit. I never could understand how people could obtain pleasure by slowly killing themselves. Sucking and exhaling smoke." He shook his head. "So! You'll want to work in stealth, I assume."

"That's right, colonel."

"There are many ways to create the illusion of accidental death. But it can take more time, and you sometimes forfeit efficiency."

"I have plenty of time. All the time in the world, colonel."

He studied me for a moment. "Yes. Yes, I see that

you do." He walked to the wall, pushed an unseen button, and a small patch of workshop floor slid open to reveal a large gunmetal-colored floor safe. He twisted the dial, pulled the door open. "I have been working on a few things which might interest you. But before we get to them, is there anything . . . more obvious . . . that you might need?"

I handed him my list. He went over it quickly. "The RDX explosives are excellent—but a little obvious. If they are detected, they would, of course, implicate a military man, or a former military man."

"I'm dealing with a mob, and wars between mobs are not all that uncommon. At any rate, I will use the explosives only when and if I have to."

He nodded, still studying the list. "Of course. The smoke bombs will be perfect for diverting attention. And you need more clips for that AK-47 of yours. A beautifully efficient weapon, but . . ."

"I have no permit for it, colonel. It can't be traced. And the Cuban army uses them."

The slightest smile crossed his face. "Forgive me, captain. You see, I am so used to command. I'm not questioning your judgment."

"I would be proud to serve under you anyplace, anytime, colonel. And I welcome your suggestions."

He nodded, reflecting for a moment. "So!" He glanced at the rest of the list. "I have all these things. You are welcome to them." He walked to his marble workbench, lighted the paper with a match, and washed the ashes down the sink. "But I have some other things I want you to look at." He reached into the floor safe and pulled out a Webber 4-B dart pistol. I recognized it from Vietnam.

"You are familiar with this, I see."

I nodded.

"Well, this one is just a little different. The one you used had twenty-six steel darts, all armed with saxitoxin. Saxitoxin is—"

"—made from the sex glands of the southern puffer—or blowfish. A deadly poison," I finished.

"Yes! But the problem with the saxitoxin is that when a medical examiner finds traces of it—especially in concert with the dart wound, which he may or may not discover—he must immediately suspect foul play. It's fine for wartime, but not ideal, I'm afraid, for these ostensibly peaceful times when an enemy's death must look . . ."

"Accidental?"

"Yes. So I have devised a new dart, a better poison. The dart is made with lignum vitae—one of the strongest woods in the world. The needle is made of superhardened glucose. The poison is from pelvic and anal spines of the scorpionfish, which, like the southern puffer, is a tropical species. But unlike the southern puffer—which can poison a person only through ingestion—the scorpionfish can sting anyone unlucky enough to pick it up, or step on it, or swim over it. The dart's needle dissolves upon the release of the poison; the dart becomes just another stub of sunken wood. And the victim immediately feels a shocking wave of pain over his entire extremity. He begins to swell, goes into convulsions, and then dies a very ugly death. Did you read about the KGB agent who had the misfortune of stepping on a scorpionfish while wading in the shallows off the Isla de Pinos in Cuba? No? Very sad. He was one of their best men— the one behind all of the problems they're now having in Haiti, I understand."

He didn't break a smile as he said it. I had always respected him, but now I felt slightly in awe of this methodical inventive genius.

"I assume it is best if the victim is stung on the feet, hands, or stomach?"

"Yes. And it is imperative they be in or near the water when they are found."

He reached into the floor safe and brought out something else. It looked like a thirteen-inch bear trap, only there were several rows of teeth. It was colored in a green-and-black camouflage design, and there were handgrips on two stocky aluminum handles.

"My God, what's . . ."

"What's this? Think back, captain. What was always the toughest strategic problem of any underwater reconnaissance? The X-factor: if your man was challenged and forced to kill, how many seconds or minutes would he have to complete his mission before the enemy challenger was found or missed?" He lifted the tooth contraption. "But this can eliminate the X-factor. Accidental death—by shark attack." Again there was the wry sharp smile. "You, above all others, should be able to appreciate this weapon, captain. You with that awful shark scar of yours. The first time I saw it, I remember thinking it was phenomenal that you survived."

Carefully, he explained the weapon to me. Hydraulic cocking device, safety, and trigger release. Made of a combination of Kevlar and aluminum—both superstrong and superlight. Teeth honed razor-sharp. It could snap an arm off or partially sever a leg.

"Death is not instantaneous," D. Harold Westervelt warned. "But if properly effected, even the victim won't know that he has been attacked by something other than a shark. I have not quite perfected it yet. I need to find a way to 'load' it with one or two actual shark's teeth so that they may be left behind in the victim's body. A small thing, but the small things often make all the difference."

He handed it to me. Very light, very strong, and very, very wicked. The ragged jumble of teeth I had seen a hundred times in the big open-water makos.

"Notice the clip, captain. It attaches easily to a weight belt. I have a couple more things you might be able to use. How about a bulletproof wet suit? Very light, very flexible."

I shook my head. "Not this time, colonel. Thanks, but no thanks."

"I hope you are not setting yourself up for sacrifice, captain."

"No. No, I'm not. I have too much work ahead of me."

"I see."

Obviously, he didn't want to hear the specifics. He

went to one of the weapon cabinets, unlocked it, and removed a weapon with which I was very familiar. The Cobra military crossbow.

"I too am an admirer of this weapon," the colonel said. "So ancient in concept, so quiet and deadly in design. It links the warriors of all time. Quite romantic, when you think about it. You know, of course, the specifics: arrow velocity of about three hundred feet per second, range of more than three hundred yards. Self-cocking mechanism. Would you like a scope?"

"No. I won't need it."

The colonel nodded. "I remember. Your work with the crossbow became almost legendary in Vietnam, did it not? What did the Marines call you? SEAL of Sherwood—"

"It doesn't matter."

"Of course. A long time ago, and a nasty little war. Some great individual bravery, but no overall bravery. None. Nothing noble about it. Not like my war. . . . Do you still have that fine Randall knife of yours?"

"Yes."

But just barely. It had taken me nearly twenty minutes of steady diving to find it after Ellsworth had been carted off by the Coast Guard. Mr. Johnson was anything but pleased at the delay. He thought it quite cruel of me. And he was probably right, but I wasn't about to lose that knife. We had been through too much together. It was my good-luck charm, and I happen to believe in good-luck charms.

D. Harold Westervelt walked me to the door.

"When does the assault take place, captain? Not where, not how—but when?"

"Very early tomorrow morning. One of them."

"Hmmm. . . . I think, captain, you should take a little bus trip tonight. Spend tomorrow in Miami, say. I have a lady friend there."

"What! I can't . . ."

He rummaged around in a nearby closet and produced a short blond toupee. "The shoulders might be a problem. Especially in warm weather. But I've encountered tougher problems of disguise—I should be able to pass for you. Elevator shoes, dark glasses, the right pads—yes, I'll have no trouble. Just let me have a quick look at your signature. Oh yes, that will be very easy. Right-handed, blocky script—the very easiest. What about a credit card? Good, I think you will sign for dinner tonight at the Fontainbleau, and be seen walking off some insomnia at . . . what time?"

"Between two and three a.m."

"Fine." There was an odd look on his face: a moistening of icy eyes, a flush of cheek. "Did you know that my late wife and I had a son, captain?"

"No," I lied. I knew, but I had never mentioned it.

"He lives in New York City, someplace. A park bench, I suppose. He left Key West when I recognized the needle tracks on his arm. I was so slow to see, but from a boy that bright, I never expected . . . Anyway, good luck on your mission, captain. I don't envy your adversaries. I don't envy them a bit."

VII

So I lay and waited off Middle Sambo Reef, lay and waited in the slow roll of midnight sea over the reef, watching the dim white shape of the cocaine boat half a mile out.

I wanted no wet suit, needed no tanks. I wore my old black Navy watch sweater, dark-blue British commando pants, black watch cap. I checked my gear. It was all at ready; all in the waterproof knapsack I would carry on my back. The Randall knife was strapped to my calf, over my pants, and Colonel Westervelt's ingenious jaws were clipped to my belt. I had the good Navy-issue mask, new Dacor TX-1000 Competition Class fins, curved open-water snorkel, and a camouflaged BC inflatable vest. Back on the little Boston Whaler was the AK-47, fully loaded this time. I hoped I wouldn't need it.

In final preparation, I painted my face and hands with black grease from the olive-drab tube, and then set out on my swim. Good tropical night for a long swim. Soft, warm wind up out of Cuba, pale moon drifting among a billion icy stars. Orion the Hunter, Taurus the Bull. Starry entertainment for a thousand generations of humanity.

A good night for swimming.

A good tropical night; the kind for romance and loving.

A fine night for killing.

I could probably have rowed the Whaler to within a quarter mile of them without much chance of being seen. But tonight I was leaving nothing to chance. Nothing. I had notified the few live-aboards at the dock that I would be away for the night. Taking a little trip, I had said. Need to get away. Going to Miami, so keep an eye on the *Sniper* for me.

They were agreeable, sympathetic.

Little did they know.

I took it slow and easy. The green glow of the Rolex watch told me that I had plenty of time. A cormorant took flight before me, paddling and splashing, struggling to be airborne. Something swirled and splashed a hundred feet or so to my right. Something big leaving a big wake.

Christ, that was all I needed—another shark.

But then I heard the familiar *poof;* the nasal exhalation of the bottle-nosed dolphin.

A good friend, the dolphin.

A good sign.

It took me just over half an hour to get to the cocaine boat. An easy, slow swim, and I arrived not even out of breath. I swam around to the bow of the boat and hung on the thick anchor line which angled off into eighty feet of onyx sea. The boat was about fifty-five feet in length; common shrimp-trawler design. It smelled of diesel fuel and the sharp iodine odor of old shrimp. Name in black-flecked paint on the bow: *Darlin' Denise.*

From within, I could hear muffled voices.

"How much longer we got . . ."

"Bastards always late . . ."

"Make a cool half mill off this shit . . ."

And then I heard something that made me strain to listen.

"Ellsworth . . . creep . . . layin' low . . ."

Laying low? He wouldn't be here tonight? Where, then?

I swam quietly to the stern. I had to get closer. I pulled myself up on the deck. I did it so slowly, so carefully, that it must have taken me five minutes. I slid across the deck on my stomach. They were in the cabin, in the dark, talking softly. I lay with my face pressed close to the damp wooden deck, warm water dripping down my nose.

"I've never liked that bastard. He gets the orders, makes us do the dirty work. Like that car business."

"So we blew up that red-headed actress bitch. Big deal man! It was a mistake—can't you get that through your head? One less snobby dame on the earth, and it doesn't bother me a bit. I hate her type, man."

"That's no shit, Stacey. Rich 'n' famous little twat

is what she was. I'm kinda glad we got her . . . Hey! Pass that rum this away once in a while."

"Well, I guess you're right, but . . . Christ, don't drink it all. Only got a bottle left!"

Soft laughter. It was all I could do to keep from barging into that cabin and killing them. Killing them slowly, making them suffer.

But then there was a fourth voice: "You young animals—you animals make me sick."

An older voice; a voice thick with disgust but edged with fear.

"What's wrong with you, Pops?"

"I got ta carry your goddamn drugs, but I ain't gotta listen to your filthy talk. I'm gonna take a walk around the deck. The stink of you three is getting' to me."

I got up on my knees, ready to move. But then there was the noise of a short scuffle, and: "Dammit, you old fool, you try that again and I'll shoot you."

"An' who's gonna pay off the Senator if you do? Huh? Oh, you won't kill me. Not yet. You'll wait until my debt's paid off to that pompous bastard, and then you'll kill me—but not *until* then. Why, if'n I was twenty years younger . . ."

"If you was twenty years younger, you'd still be in your sixties, old man!"

More laughter. More talk of great riches, more rum, flare of cigarette lighter, and I saw them. Three rough-looking men, ages between twenty-five and thirty. And the old man: stocking cap, white fishing boots, florid complexion. The biggest of the three

roughs was the one with the loud mouth, the ringleader. Black wiry hair, hooked nose, skin scarred
by acne.

When I heard the distant whine of the approaching
pickup boat, I slid past the cabin, forward, and took
good cover behind a pile of shrimp net. I was ready.
Anxious. You only fear death when you have something left to live for. They had taken the four lives
that I loved. And now, this fifth life, mine, was re-
served for vengeance.

It was the racing boat. Cigarette design, dark-blue
hull. I watched the two men climb out: the black guy,
the white guy. I had them now. I had them all—
except for Ellsworth. They still showed no lights.
They, too, were taking no chances. They, too, were
professionals.

The two new arrivals were greeted warmly by the
other three. Like a reunion. Long time no see. Been
gettin' any? How's that Campeche tail? Loud guf-
faws, lurid jokes. They went back into the cabin.

"Okay, Pop, where's the stuff?"

"You know where it is. How about my money?"

Dull thud of a heavy package being dropped upon
a table. "There it is, boys. Sixty grand, cash. Split 'er
up. Oh, and Pop— Ellsworth told me to tell you that
the Senator made a small deduction from your cut.
A ten-grand deduction."

"Ten thousand dollars!"

"Well, it sure ain't ten thousand fishes."

More laughter.

"Okay, let's get the coke loaded and get outa here.

You boys lay off shore for a couple of days. Work the nets some. Unload, go home, and then don't show your faces around Cuda Key for another two weeks. We'll be ready for another run by then."

I didn't wait to hear any more. I climbed over the shrimp net, scooted across the foredeck on my stomach, and crawled up onto the wheelhouse cabin, above them. I gave myself five minutes before I moved again. I wanted to be sure they hadn't heard me.

Okay, I was ready. I pulled two smoke bombs out of the knapsack, pulled the fuses, and tossed them forward, into the shrimp net.

Ka-wham-m-m-m!

"Jesus Christ!"

"What the hell . . ."

"The goddam boat's on fire!"

"Grab the fire extinguisher . . . get some blankets!"

They scurried out of the cabin like ants from a trodden ant hill. Dim figures spilling around on a moonlit night.

"It's up on the bow!"

When they were all forward, I dropped down off the wheelhouse behind them and hurried into the cabin. My eyes were taking their time adjusting to the deeper darkness. My knee crashed into a table; I jerked around and cracked my elbow on a cupboard. But with so much noise forward, there was no danger of me being heard. Finally, I found the money. In a canvas satchel in the corner of one of the booth seats. The radio was where I expected to find it, over the wheel. I jerked it out, letting it crash on the cabin floor.

By this time, they were starting to catch on.

"No fire out here—just smoke. What the hell's goin' on?"

Quickly I got the glass bottle of gasoline out of my bag, checked the cloth wick. In one smooth motion, I pulled open the engine hatch, lit the wick, dropped the simple little firebomb therein, and jumped.

Woosh-cra-BOOM!

"The goddam engines blew up!"

The stiletto-shaped racing boat was tethered off the stern. I cut the line with my Randall knife, then swam thirty or forty yards, pulling the sleek blue hull behind me. The trap was baited and set. I wanted them in the water. One by one, they would pay.

The fire was spreading now, blue flames roaring, eating up the old white-cypress shrimp boat. They fought it for a while: black silhouettes shimmering in reflection on the dark coral water.

And then they began to jump.

"Get to the speedboat!"

"Christ, it's not there. It's loose!"

"Out there! I see it!"

"I'm goin' back in. Gotta try to get that money!"

"Don't try it, you stupid bastard. The fuel tanks are goin' to go any second!"

But he tried anyway. I watched one of them disappear into the flames. I heard the scream, the pleas for help, the moans of a man on fire.

There would be one less for the sniper. One less for me.

The first one to reach the racing boat was an excellent swimmer. Long, smooth strokes; good rhythm—the kind you see at country-club swim meets. He was the one who had called Janet a twat. He was the one who had been glad they had killed her. I released enough breath so that I was no longer buoyant. With an upward thrust of arms, I dove. Ten, maybe fifteen feet. I released air as I went, so that I would not have to fight to stay down. I could see him coming: black, thrashing figure in the moonlight. I saw what that big dusky shark had seen. And I planned what he had planned.

When he was right above me, almost within reach of the boat, I headed up. The jaws were cocked and ready. I had never tried them. D. Harold Westervelt had warned me not to try them out of water. He had said the tremendous snap might break my wrist. I kicked as hard as I could, and the big Dacor fins drove me upward. Faster and faster. Ten feet, five feet. And I hit him with such force that it knocked him out of the water; the awful jaws snapped through his ribs as if they were autumn twigs.

"Aww-r-r-r UGH!"

In shock, he began to swim around in pathetic little circles, spitting black liquid from his mouth and nose. As he sank away into the onyx water, I pulled the lever and the jaws opened again with a hydraulic hiss.

Two more of them were coming at me. The two

from the racing boat—the black man and his white partner, the two who had been involved in Billy Mack's murder. They came thrashing along, flailing away, neither of them a good swimmer.

I hit the white guy first. Shooting along three feet underwater, I crashed into him like a torpedo. The jaws snapped onto his thigh, and I had to brace my legs against his stomach to pull them free.

"Shark! Oh, lordy, there's a shark, man . . . *my leg . . . he ate my goddam leg!"*

The black guy didn't stick around to hear the details. He swam toward the powerboat in a horrific frenzy. I surfaced behind him, took several deep bites of the warm night air, and then dove again. He was halfway onto the boat when I hit him, the jaws crushing his leg, pulling him back down into the water. I felt the flesh rip away as I pulled the lever, readying for my fourth and final victim.

I watched. And waited. The thrashing had stopped, the moans disappearing beneath the dark water. *Darlin' Denise* continued to burn, periodic explosions and the *crack* of small-arms ammunition syncopating the steady crackle of fire. In the yellow shimmer of light, I could see the old man, hands locked on a life ring, kicking his way toward the power boat.

"Pop! Pop! What's going on out there?"

The voice came from astern of the big shrimp boat. It was the man I was looking for: the ringleader. He was the big one, the careful one. The guy who had killed my wife and two sons and, only a few happy minutes before, had laughed as he called her an actress bitch.

"Sharks, I think. I think sharks got your three friends."

"Sharks . . . *Jesus* . . . well, what . . . what are we gonna do?"

"I don't know what you're gonna do, you yellow little punk, but I'm gonna try to make it to that there boat."

"But the sharks!"

"Compared to the people I've been associatin' with lately, them sharks don't scare me a bit."

So on he came, kicking away like a kid pushing a surfboard. Defiant old man who had somehow become indebted to some Senator; the Senator who owned Cuda Key and, apparently, was connected with Ellsworth and his drug ring. I had been hearing too much about that Senator lately. I would plan a meeting—but later.

When the old man was within twenty yards of me and the boat, I dove silently. I watched him pass overhead: splash of booted feet; moon shining through the round life ring. I swam on another twenty yards, surfacing close to the burning shrimp boat.

I could see the ringleader then. He sculled water, staying in one place, watching to see what would happen to Pop. And the old man got to the powerboat without incident, climbed up, and sort of shook himself like a dog.

"Sharks got the tough guy scared?" the old man cackled.

Light form the fire glimmered on the younger man's dark hair, hooked nose, and dark frightened face.

"They can get ya as easy there as they can over here! God, must be awful to have one of them big buggers hit ya. Sorta chew away at your legs! You heard the way your friends screamed, didn't ya? Well, didn't ya, ya yellow punk?"

"Pop! Start that boat and come over and get me!"

"Piddly crap! You didn't mind watchin' me swim for it! Now it's your turn!"

The old man was enjoying himself now.

"You're gonna die for this, you old scumbag. If I make it, I'll choke you to death!"

He started swimming. A slow, choppy crawl stroke, his head out of the water, turning this way and that, watching for the shark he knew was down there.

I dove, caught up with him easily, turned, and surfaced immediately in front of him.

He screamed. "Jesus God . . . what the hell? You're no . . . *who the hell are you*?"

With my tongue, I pushed the snorkel out of my mouth. I grabbed him by the shirt collar—I wanted no thumb prints on his neck. "Remember that 'actress bitch' you were talking about, asshole? I was her husband. And the father of those two kids, too."

"But how . . . hey, let's talk this over. I've got money—a lot of money—"

I turned loose of his collar and slapped him a good one. "*Shut up!* I want you to hear this before you die. I killed your friends. And I'm going to keep on killing them until they're all gone."

"But it was Ellsworth—Ellsworth's the one who set it up—I swear to God!"

"Keep talking."

The gun came up out of the water so fast that I didn't even have time to think. A little automatic; the kind you see in British spy films. But before he even had a chance to level it, I had pulled a trigger of my own. The jaws took him from the front, waist high. His eyes flashed in wide horror, his mouth agape. I pulled the jaws off, and he tried to swim away. Then he stopped, choking, and doubled up as if trying to feel, to understand how badly he had been hurt. There was a perplexed look on his face.

"You . . . you . . ."

He never finished what he was going to say. He sank away in a stream of bubbles.

I swam back toward the powerboat. The real sharks would be around by now. The big blue-water killers, the hungry ones brought in by all the blood and thrashing death.

The old man had heard what had happened.

"Hey! Hey, mister. I hope you don't think . . ."

I climbed up onto the boat. "Shut up, Pop. I'm not going to hurt you—not if you do as I say."

"Sure. Sure—you name it. Those punks deserved what you did. They had me blackmailed—"

"I don't want to hear about it. All you have to remember is this: there was an explosion, a fire. Sharks came around, but you made it." I dropped the bag of money at his feet. "Take this. It'll get you most of a new boat. Tell them the money got burned up in the fire."

"Yeah, okay. Thanks. And I want you to believe me—I'll never tell a soul. I swear to God. And that's a vow I never break."

"I would have killed you if I didn't think I could trust you. Run me halfway back to Middle Sambo and drop me off, Pop. Then hide that money—not in your house."

He looked back at the burning hulk of the shrimp boat. It was beginning to sink, hissing in its own golden reflection.

"*Darlin' Denise*—named her after my late wife. You don't have to worry, mister. That was all the home I had. By tomorrow afternoon, I'll be gone from these Keys. I was sick of 'em anyway."

VIII

The next afternoon, a bright Saturday in August, Rigaberto Herrera stopped at the docks to see me. He was in uniform—which, for him, is a three-piece suit. I sat in one of the *Sniper*'s big fighting chairs, a cold beer in my hand, working on one of the gold Penn International reels.

"Mind if I have a little talk with you, Dusky?"

"Not at all, Rigaberto. Come aboard."

He stepped across onto the stern, swung his leg over the railing, onto the deck. He took a handkerchief from his pocket and wiped the sweat from his face.

"Beer?"

He shook his head. "I'm on duty, Dusky. This is a business visit."

"Fine. Have a seat."

He sat in the plush fighting chair beside me. I told myself to be calm. I told myself how I should act, what I should say. I didn't want to be caught. I didn't want to be arrested. Not now. I needed time. A lot more time.

"Any leads on those bastards?"

Rigaberto wiped his face again. "Let's cut the act, Dusky. I've been working twenty-two hours a day since it happened, and I'm in no mood. I knew who they were; I had them spotted. Three of them. They left in a big powerboat after setting the bomb. They met a shrimp boat offshore. The *Darlin' Denise*."

"Then why aren't you out there arresting them?"

He eyed me evenly. "Don't play me for a fool, Dusky. Remember who you're talking to. I thought we were friends."

"This afternoon, apparently, you're Detective Herrera, and I'm Dusky MacMorgan, private citizen."

"Why did you do it, Dusky? I had them! Goddammit, I had them in the palm of my hand!"

"Like you had Ellsworth?"

Rigaberto slapped the arm of the fighting chair, furious. He took a deep breath, sighed. "Is that an admission of guilt?"

"I don't know what in the hell you're talking about."

He wiped his face again. He looked beat: flesh sagging beneath dark eyes; clothes that smelled sour. He had been working hard. I didn't doubt that. All day and all night long, probably. Refusing to entrust the case to anyone else, for fear of having it screwed up.

"Why don't you have something cold to drink? I'll get you some water."

He shook his head wearily. "Hell, make it a beer. I've got comp time coming. I think I'll take it now."

I got him the beer, stuck it in a Styrofoam hand cooler, and opened it with a church key. He took it gratefully.

"Jesus Christ, Dusky, I'll never figure out how you did what you did last night."

"What? I was in Miami last night."

"Oh, sure. That's what our investigation indicates. Had a man up there this morning. Big dinner at the Fontainebleau. Seen walking the lobby at sometime between two a.m. and three a.m. Used your credit card and signed for everything. Handwriting appears to match."

"And why shouldn't it?"

"Because I know you, Dusky. I know that you despise Miami. I know that that's the last place you'd go."

"Well, maybe your tastes change when you've seen your family blown to little pieces!"

Rigaberto downed half of his beer in one gulp. He looked at me wearily.

"Dusky, I loved that woman of yours. And I loved those kids. I mean that. And I mean this too: I don't blame you. But, dammit, you just can't keep on taking the law into your own hands."

"Rigaberto, I still don't know what you're talking about. What's the connection?"

"Okay. I'll play the game with you. The three men who killed your wife were on the *Darlin' Denise*. Last night, off Middle Sambo Reef, the *Darlin' Denise* caught fire. One man burned to death. We found four other bodies—all died from wounds inflicted by a shark. The only person to escape was a senile old man who talks nonsense when we try to question him."

I tried to look delighted. "They're dead? They're all dead? Good. And I hope the bastards suffered as they went down."

"How did you do it, Dusky? I can surmise how you set the *Darlin' Denise* afire. But the sharks—what did you do? Chum for an hour or two before you blew up the boat? Christ, you wouldn't have had time."

"Could that have been the cocaine boat I told you about?"

"Don't pull that innocent, blue-eyed-boy shit with me! You know it was the cocaine boat."

"Then I would have also known that the federal boys were out there waiting for them. They were, weren't they? I mean, I told them."

"They didn't believe you, or got lost, or, hell, I don't know, Dusky." Rigaberto sighed another heavy sigh. "Maybe it was an accident. Or maybe *they* set the fire and chummed up the sharks. And maybe the earth is spinning off toward the sun. Christ, I'm too tired to even think anymore."

"Probably a gang war between drug runners. That sort of thing goes on, you know."

"Gang war my ass." He sighed in surrender. And then: "Hey, get me another beer too, would you? I don't know why in the hell I didn't become a priest like my mother wanted me to be. . . ."

Gang warfare between drug runners—that's what the press called it. Romantic stuff. Terror in the tropics. Headline fare. Senators and Congressmen called for an investigation into drug-related crimes, and governors promised immediate action. After a few weeks, it all died down, and no one really cared anymore. A few drug runners were killed by sharks—so what? Who needs 'em?

And after a week or so, after the reporters went home, and the politicians started focusing on more important matters—like how to get reelected—the big drug boats started to make their scheduled runs to the Bahamas and Mexico and South America, and people in high places started turning their heads once again, their hands outstretched for bribes, because there is, after all, big money in drugs. And supply the demand is the American way of life.

Like the drug runners, I too lay low for a while. I worked on the *Sniper*. I had her hauled, and spent a long dirty afternoon scraping her clean and repainting her with the very, very best antifouling paint. And while I painted her bottom, Hervey Yarbrough, who owns the boat ways up at Cow Key, painted her upper hull and flybridge.

"You want it what color, Dusky?"

"Blue-black, Hervey. A deep-water shade of blue-black."

"Well, I'll do her, dern it—but ain't nobody gonna be able to spot this vessel o' yourn after dark. God he'p ya if'n ya break down out in the Stream some afternoon. They won't fin' ya till ya drift halfway ta England!"

Hervey muttered and grumbled and second-guessed all afternoon. A good man, Hervey Yarbrough. Born of shipbuilder stock that had come to Key West in the early 1800s, he was an authentic Conch—which is what the old white islanders are called. Hervey's people lived in Key West during the era in which changing channel markers, so that the incoming ships would go a wreck on a reef, was common practice. They would lure the ships aground, go out and help save the ship and the ship's manifest, then claim a percentage of the cargo in the infamous Key West salvage courts. In those times, Key West and the Dry Tortugas were not favorite ports of call with the world's oceangoing captains.

They called the Conchs who practiced such piracy "wreckers" and "moonrakers," and they were actually licensed by the courts. Licensed not to change channel markers, but to salvage cargo and go to the aid of reefed vessels. In 1835 there were twenty such licensed wreckers operating out of Key West. Hervey was a descendant of Captain S. Sanderson, master of the schooner *Orion*.

"But he weren't no moonraker, no sirree," Hervey told me as we painted. "A good honest man, he was. Lotta them pirates in back times—"

"—and a lot now."

"Dern if tha' ain't the truth! But our family weren't no moonrakers. Good honest wreckers, we was. An' those backtime wreckers worked for their money, by gum. Goin' out to the reefs to rescue men 'n' ships with one o' them blowin' blue northers. Day or night; didn't matter. Lost a few, saved a few. But by gum they worked for what th' courts give 'em. They was good brave seafarin' men."

I needed the day of hard work and hot sun; a day around good people like Hervey and his wife and pretty teenage daughter. I had been a walking corpse for days. I saw, but could not see. I heard, but could not hear. Everything was in black and white; the faces of strangers passed on the streets were shrouded by a white corona, the film of death. The chatter of birds, the moan of south wind in Australian pines, the barking of stray dogs, all came to me as a dreamy echo; the remembrance of another life to someone trapped in a gauzy netherworld.

Coming back from Middle Sambo Reef that night had not been easy. I was no longer the hunter, I was the hunted. Too much death, too much horror, too many screams that would reverberate forever in my mind. I came close to the edge. Too close. Halfway back to Key West, I had pulled the Whaler back to idle, then switched the little fifty-horse engine off. Drifting, I had watched the dim blaze of lights which shrouded the string of Keys, trailing off to the northeast like a comet's tail.

Why should I go on? What more was there to do?
They had killed four of me. I had killed six of them,
and was responsible for the fiery death of another.

What was left?

I thought of Janet; thought of my two fine young
sons. They had never had a chance. Never had a
chance to see life; to learn to love the good and true
things as I had.

And with their deaths, all of my appreciation of
life had died with them.

Was there any purpose in an existence dedicated
to mindless vengeance? To mindless killing?

No. Vietnam had proved that to me, and to too
many others.

Why function in a mindless world with an insane
mission?

Slowly, I had picked up the AK-47: wood forearm
and metal butt plate cold in my hands. I slid a cartridge into the chamber and placed the barrel of the
weapon against my forehead, the butt of the rifle
angled solidly against the fiberglass deck.

I knew I could do it.

There was no fear, no trembling hands.

I placed my thumb against the trigger of the brutal
automatic—and that's when I heard the familiar *poof*
of a dolphin. Bottle-nosed dolphins: a family of them.
They circled near the skiff, diving and rising like
merry-go-round creatures. Side by side, up and
down, up and down, in tight formation. A protective
formation. One for all, and all for one. Perfect creatures in grand design.

And in some strange way, that was affirmation enough.

I had lost my family unit; lost them to the mindless ones.

I would not let them take me, too.

There would be other people, other families who needed help. There had always been the pirates, the soulless moonrakers of humanity; those who leached the money and the lives of the innocent. My death would serve only them. But my life—my life could make them sorry they were ever born.

So I sat and watched the dolphins. Clear night, moon setting in the west. Soft wind, open expanse of dark sea. They would kill me. In time, I would die by their hands. Because wherever they were, wherever they killed and robbed and bullied, I would be. Death on my mind and them in my sights. . . .

After another two days of hard work, and of draining the bulk of the money left in our bank account, the *Sniper* was ready to go.

I had had her tuned to perfection, and added a Si-Tex radar system. The antenna had been mounted forward of the fly-bridge, and the radar screen itself was bolted above the cabin controls. It produced a clear, twelve-inch image with a range up to forty-six miles. The existence of distant vessels came to me as little lime-green bleeps on the sweep of screen.

"Sure look pretty, don't she?" Hervey had said, admiring his own brushwork. "With that blue-black upper, the light-blue bottom paint and the gold waterline, she look pretty as a pitchure, huh?"

She did indeed look fine. In a burst of characteristic generosity, Hervey's wife had worked overtime to surprise me. With her considerable artistic talent, she had painted "*Sniper—Key West, Florida*" in small white script on the stern.

"Hope you don't mind, Cap'n MacMorgan, but I thought it would look nice," she had said.

And I smiled—smiled for the first time in more than a week.

She added, "Janet, your kids—I sure was awful sorry to hear about them. They was so good. They say us Conchs is cliquish, but I liked that woman the moment I met her. We ain't standoffish when it comes ta good people. And I just want you to know that if'n there's anythin' you need—ever—you got friends on this island. Like tha' business off Middle Sambo th' other night? Well, had you needed any help, my old man an' a buncha other Conchs woulda slipped out there with ya. We take care of our own, we do. Always have, always will. I just wanted ya to know. . . ."

I didn't ask her what she had heard, how she had found out. The few true islanders that are left have their own ways of knowing. Something about her concern, her affection for Janet, her way of telling me that they would help—no matter what—touched me. Really touched me. I winked, said nothing, and I managed to hold back the hot rush of tears until I was offshore, well away from Cow Key. . . .

*   *   *

There was a guy waiting for me when I got back to the docks. I nosed the *Sniper* around, port engine forward, starboard engine in reverse, then backed her in, stopped my sternway with a forward thrust of power, then shut her down.

"Are you Captain Henry MacMorgan?"

"That's right." I looked up briefly as I made the lines fast and rigged the spring line. He was a big man in a neat business suit. Short black hair, angular face: the Clint Eastwood type, only burlier.

He took a wallet from his jacket pocket, opened it, and held it up plainly for me to see. "My name's Fizer, Captain MacMorgan. Norm Fizer. I'm with the federal government."

"Great. Enjoy the benefits. Buy more suits."

"I think we might have met before, Captain Mac-Morgan. Remember, Dusky?"

I stood up and studied his face. And, finally, I did remember. Stormin' Norman. Special Forces. CIA, maybe. One hush-hush mission and too many jungle nights in Cambodia, long, long ago. A good man that we all had entrusted with our lives. And he had come through—unusual for a government man in those times. And these times. And all times.

"No," I lied. "Can't say as I do."

He smiled. "Guess I can't remember, either. Mind if I come aboard and we talk about our poor memories?"

We sat in the forward salon, me with Hatuey, him with ice water and a squeeze of lime.

"I told that Lenze character everything I know

about the murder of my friend, Norm, so if that's why you're here . . ."

He held up his hands. "Hold it, Dusky. Not so fast. Give me a chance to set a few things straight, first, and then we'll talk. Okay?"

"Sure."

He sipped at his lime and water. "Before you resigned from the Navy, you had a very high security clearance. That's why we were together in that place neither of us can remember. A very high security clearance, and so, back then, I could have prefaced what I am now about to say with 'Restricted Information' and gone on with every assurance that you would not blab, and get me fired and force me into selling that crummy secondhand heap that my wife drives. Now I have to ask you for your word." He chuckled. "How about it, Dusky? A few minutes of talk, all strictly confidential."

"You're not here, right?"

"Correct. I'm up in Atlanta this very moment—just as you were up in Miami one Friday night—"

"Now hold it, Fizer!"

He waved his hands at me, relaxed, self-assured. "I didn't come here to entrap you, Dusky. Take it easy. We're on the same side."

"And what side is that?"

"Oh, the side of law, order, and justice for all, of course! But all sarcasm aside, Dusky, I . . . well . . . we need your help."

I set down the Hatuey bottle and looked him straight in the eye. Brown eyes. Serious, dark eyes deep-set within the fraternity-boy face. "Why should I help you? Your people didn't exactly put a lock on one Benjamin Ellsworth. Where in the hell were your people when he was planning to put a bomb in my car? A car which just happened to be holding my wife and kids when it blew up!"

He lowered his eyes. "I know, I know—that's why I'm down here, Dusky. And I'm sorry, I truly am. We've got problems in the department. We've been having people go bad. People in high places. It's money, Dusky. Big money. And the weak ones can't resist it. Would you believe that I myself was offered a quarter million in cash just to turn my head once? Just *once*."

"So what happened?"

His eyes focused, his nostrils flared. This was the guy I had known in Cambodia. "That fellow is taking a nice little vacation in federal prison. And he spent the first two weeks in court hobbling around on crutches. Okay?"

"You made your point, Norm."

"So how about it, Dusky? Come back into the fold."

"I don't like wearing a suit."

"We have too many people who wear suits already. We want someone who knows boats, knows the water, and can take care of himself—and that's you. You'll still run your charter business. But every now and then I might drop you the word, and then you'd tell your friends that you're leaving on a little vacation cruise. We'll back you, we'll finance you— but you take orders from us."

"And what if, on one of these little assignments, I get into trouble?"

"It'll be like the other place neither of us were—you have to fight your way out—or die trying. Because we'll disavow all knowledge of your activities."

"And what about the local law?"

"I'll take care of that."

"And what if I say no?"

"Then I'm afraid we'll have to let Mr. Lenze—who is headed for a hard fall very soon, incidentally—continue his investigation into the murder of five drug runners, all of whom had records longer than both of our arms. By the way, the way you treated the old man impressed us. We made him give back the money, of course, but your sympathetic treatment—well, it helped us make the final decision."

"Give me a day to think it over, Norm."

"Fine, Dusky. But we need you. We need someone with local cover who can work fast and clean. Battles between mobsters have a way of exposing the soft underbelly of crime rings to federal three-piece-suit men like me. It wouldn't be the first time we've used someone like you."

He finished his lime and water, stood up, and held out his hand. "By the way, I have a message for you—Colonel Westervelt says you should keep the little toys he gave you. He hopes you'll be needing them soon."

"I hardly know the guy."

"*Right*. And I love Atlanta in August. Dusky, he's the one who shoved this whole thing through."

IX

I was glad the dogs guarding Cuda Key were Dobermans. The Doberman is a singularly merciless animal—but with one major flaw. They are so anxious to attack an intruder that they often fail to bark a warning first.

I could not afford to have any warnings sounded.

It was a full-moon midnight. I worked my way through the jungle of mangroves off Bahia Honda Key, slapping at the vectoring mosquitoes. An occasional car roared over the high arching bridge behind me, straightening and slowing for the narrow, seven-mile ordeal which would carry them to Marathon. A weekday night at midnight—one of the few fairly safe times to travel that deadly Florida Keys Highway, A1A. Few drunks, fewer tourists.

Earlier, I had made a partial reconnaissance of the area by car. Reconnaissance by day in preparation for the reconnaissance by night. Cuda Key lay about

a mile off Bahia Honda in the clear, calm water of
Florida Bay. From the shore, I had made notes: a
broad-shouldered tourist writing postcards in the hot
sun. A hundred acres of island, with plenty of cover.
Gumbo limbo, bamboo, Jamaican dogwoods, bayonet
plants and pepper trees. Big house on a shell mound,
nearly hidden by trees, and squat like a fortress,
made of coquina rock. Deepwater entry on the Big
Spanish Channel side. Neat docks with two big cruis-
ers, several smaller boats—and one dark-blue
cigarette-style hull. Smaller outbuildings, a steel-
mesh fence surrounding the island, and the trotting
Dobermans. That's all I could see—from the road.
Now my little Boston Whaler was tethered to its anchor in the shallows of a jungled spoil bank, and I
moved toward the island which housed members of
one of the Keys' bigger drug rings. And, I hoped,
the man who had masterminded the deaths of my
wife and sons.

I pulled the black watch cap down over my forehead and ears, spat in and rinsed my mask, then
adjusted it on my face.

I carried only two real weapons: my Randall knife,
and the Webber 4-B dart pistol. But the lignum vitae
darts were not armed with the scorpionfish poison.
Instead, they held a simple tranquilizer—one that
would knock a big dog out for an hour, or a medium-
sized man for approximately half that time.

I was working for the government now. Doing it
their way. And Stormin' Norman had forbidden me
to kill—unless I absolutely had to.

It had not gone over well with me.

"We need to build a better case, Dusky. More proof."

"I've got all the proof I need, for God's sake."

"Great! We'll just subpoena them all into federal court, have you stand up and tell the judge your story, and then he'll lock them all away for a hundred years. Dusky, it's not that damn simple. We need a little illegal bugging done. When we find out who is in on it, how long it has been going on, what the connections are and when their next score is, *then* we'll get the warrants."

"And what if you can't get the warrants?"

"If the rot goes *that* deep, then we'll turn you loose. My God, don't grin like that, captain. You look like the grim reaper himself when you grin like that."

So instead of the RDX explosives, I carried four candy-colored and candy-sized bugging devices. My mission was to gain access to the island, place the bugs in strategic areas, then escape without anyone knowing that I had been there.

It sounded easy enough.

I slid into the water, noiseless as a seal, and began the half-mile swim. I could have walked most of the way. Except for the passes and the channels and a few potholes where the big flats fish and barracuda covey on low spring tides, Florida Bay is shallow. It is a vast littoral zone that is gravid with life: everything from mud worms to tunicates to bonefish to sharks.

The full moon cast a frosted pale sheen across the

water and veiled Cuda Key in a silver mist. I had spent the previous day reading everything I could about the island. Two thousand years of human inhabitation. First, the prehistoric Tequesta or Calusa Indians. They were expert fishermen and seamen. They carved beautiful wooden masks and idols and made sacrifices to their nature gods. By canoe, they traded with the Indians of Cuba and South America, and they were such fierce warriors that they extracted tribute from the other Indians of Florida, and they held the Spaniards—with their steel swords and shields—at bay for more than a hundred years. But finally, not the swords of the Spanish but the diseases of the Spanish caught up with them. And drove them to extinction. Now all that remained of those Indians were the high shell mounds which they had built—like the mound which foundationed that fortress of a stone house. A Spanish mission came later. And then Cuda Key became a hideout for pirates. And after the American men-of-war routed the pirates, the island became the home of fishermen, and then a citrus farmer, then a goat herder, then a group of nudists trying to breed their own superrace, and, finally, pirates again.

These were the pirates that I hunted.

I made good time in the calm night water. Mullet streamed and jumped in the shallows beside me, and I heard something big—a barracuda, probably—knifing the baitfish somewhere beyond, in the ocean darkness.

I chose an area of the island where the mangroves

hung out over the water for my point of entry. I slid up the bank, climbed quietly along the arching roots. I took off my mask and fins and hid them. The western edge of the big house lay high before me. There was one light on—a bedroom light, probably. I forced myself to keep a mental map as I moved along, planning alternate routes of escape in my head. It was a good feeling I had; an old familiar feeling. And once you know it, you never forget it. Ever. A chemical nervousness low in the stomach; steady pulse of blood mixed with adrenaline. Controlled breathing, soft and shallow. All senses alerted, ready. Hearing, acute; eyes that sweep and take in everything.

I was the silent one.

The night stalker; the midnight hunter.

And once you have done it well and loved it, you never stop loving it.

I reached a broad clearing which bordered the steel fence. In the military, we had called such a clearing a "killing area." I kept low, on my stomach. I felt beggar lice and sandspurs latch into my hands, my black sweater, the soft British commando pants. I knew what I needed to get across that fence. And, finally, I found it.

A big gumbo limbo tree, looking amber in the moonlight, reached one thick limb over the fence. The fence itself would have been easy enough to climb or to cut, but it might have been electrified, or wired for sound. I wanted to take no chances. From one of the leg pockets of the commando pants, I took out a thirty-foot length of half-inch, five-strand rope.

I tossed it over the limb, caught the other end, and tied a quick loop, using a bowline. I pulled the other end through until the knot was snug against the limb. I climbed the rope, hand over hand. The limb sagged beneath my weight, but not enough to touch the fence. When I was safely in the tree, I backed the knot out, coiled the rope, and stuck it back in my pants.

I waited for the Dobermans to come.

They were wind trackers. They needed no ground scent.

And come they did. On a run.

And barking.

"Dammit!"

They gathered beneath the tree like coonhounds. There were three of them. Two big black ones, and another that was cinnamon-colored. They jumped at me, trying to get up the tree: snarling, teeth snapping, looking like animal devils with their pointed ears, broad chests, and stiletto faces.

A floodlight switched on at the house up on the mound. A figure appeared.

"What in the hell are those dogs up to, Jimmy?"

And from a little cottage at the base of the mound came another voice.

"Jes' goin' out to check, Senator!"

I watched the second figure walk toward me.

"Snake Eyes! Gator! What ya got, boys?"

I had an idea. I could dart the caretaker with no problem. But then they would know that I was there. Quietly, I cleared my throat. A cat doesn't meow.

Not at night. And certainly not when three Dobermans are after it.

"E-e-e-auw-O-O-O!"

A high, soprano wail—like a small panther.

"Aw, shit!"

"E-e-e-auw-O-O-O-O!"

"Rusty! You boys come away from that damn cat! They got a cat, Senator!"

"A cat! Oh, Jesus. Well, I didn't pay two thousand dollars for trained cat killers!"

"Tol' you we shoulda got shepherds! You can trust a shepherd—but those bastards . . ."

"Pull them away, Jimmy. I'm trying to get some work done up here."

"Christ, Senator, they turn on me when they're like that! Don't trust 'em, no sir!"

"Okay, okay. Let them eat the cat, for all I care. But if they aren't quiet in five minutes, it's your job!"

The caretaker called to the dogs for a while, then headed back toward his cottage, muttering. "Goddam Dobermans . . . don't know why they can't use retrievers . . . good Chesapeake 'ould eat all three o' their asses, then lick me like a puppy. . . ."

I darted them. One by one. Soft whimpers, heavy, drunken thud of collapsing dogs.

I swung off the limb and dropped to the ground. I had an hour before they woke up. Maybe more, maybe a little less.

From tree to tree, from shadowed bush to shadowed bush I went. At the little caretaker's cottage, I paused, my eye to the corner of the window. He sat within in a soft chair, reading an article in a fishing magazine. He held an old pipe in his right hand, the stem repaired with electrical tape. I moved up the shell mound, mindful of my footing, toward the big house.

The bedroom light was still on. I peered in. At first I thought the room was empty. But then a bathroom door opened, and I saw the woman. Tall ebony Negress. She wore a filmy nightgown. Small, sharp thrust of dark breasts plainly visible beneath the gown. She moved in front of the big floor lamp, and I saw the flat stomach, the perfect curve of rounded Negro hips vee away into black thatch. She was beautiful: short cropped hair, face the color of certain autumn leaves. Fluidly, she walked across the room, switched on the stereo, and made herself a drink at the bar. Bourbon and Bach.

Keeping in the shadows of the big house, I moved around to the side door. Big door, black mahogany. Little rows of numbered buttons were placed where the doorbell should have been. An electronic lock. I retraced my steps, back along the house, and tried the door from which the Senator had exited and reentered. More glowing buttons. I tried the door anyway, and to my surprise, it swung open. I stuck my hand in.

Dark living room. Marble statues like mannequins on the plush carpet. I could hear the soft music coming from the bedroom. And from another room the deep voices and hushed laughter of men talking.

I slipped in and closed the door behind me. From my pocket I took a Wise high-intensity penlight. Waterproof, it threw a laserlike beam when you screwed the lens down. I checked two tables before I finally found the phone. I switched on the tiny light, removed the transmitter, and unscrewed the red power wire and the green and yellow ground wires. I added the bug, replaced the phone. It would pick up all phone conversations on that line, and any conversations which took place in the living room.

I crept down the dark hallway toward the bedroom. The music still played, but there was no band of light beneath the door. I waited, I listened. And finally I took a chance. I had to place a bug in the master bedroom. I opened the door ever so slowly and, on my belly, crawled in.

Soft, steady inhalations and exhalations came from the long dark figure in the bed. Moonlight filtered in the two French windows, and in that soft glow I searched for a place to hide another little transmitter.

There was a broad hatchcover bedroom table at the foot of the bed. I crawled toward it.

"Darling? Senator, is that you?"

I flattened, trying not to breathe, trying to will the loud beating of my own heart to stop.

I heard the rustle of covers as she sat up.

"Is someone there?"

Soft lilt of British West Indies accent.

I gave it a full five minutes before I allowed myself to move again. I stuck the little bug beneath the bottom surface of the heavy table with an ingenious sound-sensitive plaster the colonel had devised. It had the texture and color of old chewed gum.

I gave it another ten minutes of dead silence, then crawled from the room. Once in the hallway, with the door closed behind me, I pulled up the sleeve of my watch sweater and checked the luminous green glow of the Rolex. Twelve-fifty-two. I had about twenty minutes before the Dobermans woke up.

The men were still in the room talking. Soft deep voices, businesslike. The meeting room: probably den or library. I lay with my ear to the door, hearing snatches of conversation.

"Pay off . . . Cleveland . . . wants too big a cut . . ."

"Maybe, plane crash . . ."

"Bahamas . . . getting easier . . . heroin . . ."

Three voices. One vaguely familiar—but not Ellsworth's. I knew Ellsworth's unique intonations all too well.

I had to get a bug into that room.

But how? Their meeting might take five more minutes, or five more hours.

I decided to give them a little more time.

I moved down the hallway, hoping that there would be a second entrance to the large master bathroom, and there was. It was halfway to the end, off to the right. I switched on the little flashlight. The place was as big as a boat. Sunken tub, gold-plated faucet fixtures, mirrors on the ceiling, redwood sauna bath. I opened the door of the sauna bath. I had planned on putting the bug near the sink. That's the common ploy when important, deadly things are discussed: go into the bathroom, turn on both spigots, and talk. But the sauna bath might be even better.

I didn't know how the little transmitter would react to extreme heat, so I placed it under one of the long benches, away from the rock-covered heater.

That done, I moved back down the hallway.

And still they talked. I checked my watch. Five more minutes, tops. I had to think of a way to get the bug into that room. I didn't want to be trapped by those dogs again. Perhaps I should have killed them. No—then they would have known; been on guard forever afterward.

And finally it came to me.

A dangerous idea—but necessary.

I crept back out to the living room and found the main bar. What do the wealthy ones like to drink? I made three strong bourbons, on the rocks. I found a small vase of silk flowers. I removed the flowers, deposited the bug, then put the flowers back in. I put the drinks and the flowers on a silver tray. Back in the hallway, I listened to make sure they were still talking.

They were.

I placed the tray by the door, found the hallway light, and switched it on.

And then I knocked: a soft feminine knock, three times.

"What?"

I knocked again, and then took cover.

I heard the door open; smelled the odor of the expensive cigars.

"I told you I didn't want to be bothered, Bimini— hey, what's this?"

I heard the rattle of glasses as he picked up the tray.

"Hey, three fresh bourbons."

"Doesn't she know I don't drink?"

"What the hell. She's been drinking herself. Didn't I tell you she takes better care of me than any white woman I ever had? And flowers, too." He called down the hall toward the bedroom, "Thank you, darling. Be with you as soon as I can!"

The door closed amid bawdy male laughter.

The glasses and tray would be taken away in the morning.

The flowers would stay.

I hoped.

I switched off the light. She would have switched it off before her final trip to the bedroom. And then I made my way out of the house.

So far, everything had gone perfectly. Without a hitch.

Just like old times. I thought of Billy Mack. He loved night maneuvers. There had been no one better than he in the jungle. At night. When the killing or the reconnaissance had to be done silently. He had grown up on a farm and had spent half of his life in the woods.

We used to talk about our boyhoods on those god-awful rain-forest nights, waiting in the muck of those coffee-colored rivers, waiting to kill or be killed. I had told him about traveling with the circus. It turned out that our paths had actually crossed earlier. His folks had carted him clear to Toledo so that he might see the show under the big top.

"Christ, I remember you now! That blond head of yours swinging back and forth with all those good-looking Italian people. Shit, I can't believe it! I thought you was the luckiest kid on earth. Traveling like that."

"I was, Billy. For a long time I was. . . ."

Funny, the things you remember about old, lost friends. He told me once about the time he had picked up the trail of a big buck. He had done everything just right. Figured out where the buck was going. Crossed the trail and moved to that spot, keeping well downwind.

"I came through some bushes, movin' quiet, and I'll be damn if that big ol' buck wasn't standin' right there. It was like I knew the way of the woods as well as he did, to intercept him like that. H was a beauty, too. A fine-looking rack of antlers—a twelve-pointer. He stood there, nose kind of quiverin', those big brown eyes lookin' fierce and proud. I raised my gun ever so slowly and . . . and . . ."

"And what, Billy?"

"I couldn't shoot, Dusky." His voice was soft, reflective. "He was just too . . . too fine . . ."

Billy Mack had known the woods. And the jungle. He couldn't be surprised in the woods. But on the

sea, on a clear August day, when all boaters are supposed to be comrades . . .

Quietly, I made my way down the shell mound.
The caretaker's light was still on. I glanced inside.
The magazine had been placed facedown on the
chair. The pipe still smoldered.

Where had he gone?

To the bathroom, probably. I checked my watch.
It was after one a.m.

I retraced my earlier route, staying in the shadows
of trees and bushes. The big gumbo limbo was in
front of me. I stopped and checked to make sure the
dogs were still there.

They were: three sleeping figures looking black in
the silver moonlight. I got the rope out of my pocket.
My clothes were still clammy. I was beginning to
smell: the deep musk of wet wool and sweat. I
needed a shower and a cold beer. Only a half-mile
swim and a long, pretty boat ride to go.

I tossed the rope up over the lowest big limb. I
fixed the knot. I was home free, now.

I pulled myself up, up, but whirled around when
I heard a noise behind me.

The dogs waking up?

No, a man. Something in his hand, Something big,
like a bat. And in that fleeting moment in the gauzy
moonlight, I recognized the face. A face I knew and
hated.

Just before my head exploded, I recognized the
face of Benjamin Ellsworth.

X

The ebony woman stood over me when I awoke for the second time. She wore a long cotton print skirt with blue conch shells and green hibiscus blooms on it. Her blouse was of a white satinlike material, and she wore no bra beneath it.

"What . . . where the hell am I?"

I tried to sit upright, but she forced me back down on the bed with surprising ease. She shook her head and held a brown index finger to her lips. I was not to speak. There was a basin of water and a sponge on the table beside the little cot on which I lay. She wiped my face with the cool water.

"You've been badly injured, captain," she whispered. "For two days and two nights I thought you would certainly die."

"*Two days!*"

Softly, she covered my mouth with her hand. It smelled faintly of spice; some strange perfume.

She whispered again. "If they hear you, captain, they will come and question you. They will try to force you to talk, and you are still not well."

I closed my eyes and knew that she was right. My neck ached, my head throbbed with every heartbeat, and the room spun in the self-imposed darkness. I opened my eyes. So I was still alive. It came as some surprise. I had awoken at some other time. That night or the previous night—I didn't know. Everything was blackness. A total and complete absence of all light, and I was sure that I was dead. In limbo, perhaps. Or hell. Yes, hell, because that's what I deserved. I had killed too often, and too well. . . .

"The gauze around your head is filled with moss. Don't let it frighten you, captain. It's an old island cure that I know. I'm afraid we have no real medical facilities here. And the Senator forbade the summoning of a doctor."

I touched the bandage that was wrapped around my skull. It felt hot and wet. I looked at my fingers. Blood.

I saw the tremor of concern cross her face. She began wiping me with the sponge again. "You really are much better. You must believe that, captain. It's very important that you not let yourself die. Very important."

She looked tired. Very tired—as if she hadn't slept for days.

"You've been with me the whole time?" I asked in a hoarse whisper.

"Yes. Mr. Ellsworth wanted to kill you. And he

would have. But they found some sort of electronic device that they think you planted here. The Senator insisted on questioning you. He's worried. They will make you tell them everything, and then kill you. That is the truth. Please believe me."

Oh, I believed her all right. Beneath the white sheet, I tested the rest of my body. Arms and legs okay. My left ankle hurt a little—I had, perhaps, twisted it in falling. But my head felt as if someone had stuffed shattered glass in through my ears.

She saw me take the quick survey, and mistook my concern.

"Yes, you're naked." Her cheeks turned a delicate auburn color as she seemed to blush. "The Senator was quite upset when he realized that I had undressed you. He is quite jealous of anyone who . . . who looks better than he does. But don't let it bother you. I was a nurse before I came here. A very good nurse. Sometimes I wonder why I ever let myself . . ."

Her voice trailed off, leaving a strangely tangible sadness afloat in the little room. I seemed to be in some kind of basement. The first basement I had ever seen in Florida. No windows, plumbing fittings and electrical conduit overhead, cool concrete walls. Without moving my head, I could see a shelf of radio apparatus in front of me. On a cork board was a large nautical chart of the Florida Keys, and another of the Bahamas. There were little red pins stuck in the charts. What did they mark? Pickup points?

"I have some broth you should try to get down,"

the woman said. She produced a stoneware bowl and a big spoon. Gently, she added another pillow beneath my head. It was some kind of beef soup. I realized that I was starving. She couldn't spoon it fast enough.

"Slowly, captain, slowly. You've been sick for some time."

And then my stomach rolled. Nausea. She saw it coming and forced my head into her lap.

"Don't be embarrassed, captain. Let it come."

She held me gently, talked to me in soothing tones. Bile and vomit on the pretty dress. I wanted to apologize, but I couldn't speak. I was racked by convulsions, and there was a knife in my brain, and then, gratefully, there was darkness . . . a darkness that echoed with someone whispering in my ear: "You must get well, captain . . . you must get well and take me away from this awful, awful place. . . ."

More voices. A voice that I recognized and loved. It was Janet. She stood before me in the darkness, calling to me. She wore the Irish twill suit and white blouse she had worn in her last movie. I had never seen her so beautiful. An ethereal light seemed to glow within her face and long auburn hair. She held out a long white hand to me.

"Dusky! Come on! We've been waiting and waiting. . . ."

Dazzling smile on the happy face. It was as if she was waiting for me to run across the moor with her.

Across the moor . . .

I wanted to go; wanted to go so badly. I struggled in the darkness. My feet wouldn't move, my mouth wouldn't open to reply, my lungs refused even to breathe. She was just over *there;* a few steps beyond the veil. I fought and fought to join her, and still my traitor body would not budge.

And then Ernest and Honor were there, too. Blond hair as white as pure sunlight. They giggled and called to me. And when I did not answer, they grew sober. They exchanged looks and, as if upon cue, they straightened and saluted me, like little West Point cadets.

I wanted to go to them so badly. I wanted to cross the line. I felt as if I wanted to die. . . .

Yellow light and soft bursts of color beyond my eyelids.

More voices:

"I tell you, that big bastard is never going to wake up. It's been three days, and I say let's go ahead and get rid of him."

"Well, I don't give a damn what you say, Ellsworth. I'm tired of getting you out of jams. He knows something. Those bugs were state department bugs. And if he was sent here by the government, I have to know what they're up to. I want to know for sure before I make final arrangements for South America."

"He was after *me,* Senator. And if Jimmy and I hadn't found those dogs, I'm telling you—"

"You're not telling me anything, Ellsworth. I'm

telling you. We'll give him another day or two. And if he's not well enough to talk then, then we'll get Lenze to set something up and make it look like an accident. But I'm not going to hand him over to you just for your personal amusement."

I heard footsteps going toward the door, and I heard the door open. I heard someone take two steps back toward my bed, and I felt the wet stringer slide down my face. Before turning out the lights, Ellsworth had spat on me. . . .

It was Janet again. She stood on the bow of my old cruiser, *Striker*, face into the wind, hair streaming out behind her, just as she had that first time.

We had met the week before. Her film company had chartered my boat to take them around scouting locations. They wanted a deserted place with a beach and palm trees, clear water and shallow coral reefs.

I had taken them out to a little spot I knew off the Content Keys. It was everything they wanted and more.

You hear a lot about "positive chemistry" between two people.

And I had never really believed in it—until I met her.

Of course, it was expected of me. Every man who had ever met her or ever seen her on the screen felt it.

The unusual thing was that she had felt it for me. And I knew it. She let me know it.

Nothing flirty, nothing coy. She displayed her interest through questions and conversation, direct gazes and an occasional bawdy wink. When we passed each other on the narrow confines of the *Striker*, we always seemed to brush closer than necessary. There was an intense, physical awareness of each other between us, no doubt about that. But there was something more, too.

She was the one who finally broke the ice. Frankly, I have always been a little shy of women. Not intimidated, not lacking in confidence—but just reluctant to get involved in that long tiresome game of "Is he going to try to take me to bed?" and "Will she let me take her to bed?"—the big questions of dating sexuality that always, always get in the way of interesting talk and genuine friendship between a man and a woman.

So she made the first move.

I was down on the docks, coiling lines. I smelled of fish and, after a long day on the boat, my hair was bleached to straw and my face was peeling.

She came down to the boat in long, mannish strides. She wore baggy brown fishing pants belted tight to the narrow waist, and a baggy blue shirt that seemed to make her blue eyes glow like a certain shade of Gulf Stream water. She looked great.

"How about it, sailor? Interested in a good time?" She had her hands on her hips and punctuated the questions with a big wink, the way a dishwater blonde in a 1930s movie might have.

"You dames are all alike," I had said, playing the role. "Coupla quick drinks an' ya try to push us swabbies inta the sack."

The ice broken, we both fell into fits of laughter.

"How about it, Dusky? Buy a dead-tired actress dinner?"

"Dutch treat, maybe," I had said, still laughing. "Just give me a minute to shower."

"Naw, you look fine. My grandfather was an old Iona Banks fisherman out of Scotland. It'll be nice to go out with a man who doesn't smell like the latest French perfume."

So we went out. That night and every night afterward. And we had great long rambling conversations. Boats, books, politics. I told her about the circus, a little bit about what I had done in the Navy, and a lot about me. She told me about acting, about growing up in New York City, and how she was ready for something different; something lasting.

Two opposites. Two people made for each other.

We held hands occasionally, but I never once tried to kiss her. I enjoyed the woman; I enjoyed the person—and I didn't want it suddenly complicated or spoiled.

Then one late evening, almost midnight, I had heard a hesitant knock at my cabin door. It was Janet. She was in tears. She took two steps and fell into my arms.

"Dusky, I can't stand it anymore. I can't! All those silly takes and retakes. It's all so important to them, and it all seems so silly to me."

I had gotten her a beer and left her alone while she showered and settled down. I cast off the lines and headed out the old Northwest Channel into the tranquilizing darkness of night sea. Three miles, four miles: far away from the pressures of celluloid and make-believe, far away from the bright Key West lights. And then I shut the engines down, drifting. I looked at the stars and thought about what I wanted to do with my life. A professional killer looking for a purpose. And after I had decided, I went down to her. I expected a dramatic proposal, well-rehearsed jubilation afterward.

But there was none of that. She lay asleep in the forward cabin, fist to her mouth like a child.

Quietly, I slipped off my shoes, my shirt, and lay down beside her and was soon asleep.

I don't know who awoke first. Maybe her, maybe me—or maybe together. But our mouths were already joined; open and searching the other. In feverish readiness, we wrestled each other's clothes off. Her breasts, her hips, her silken hair—the most beautiful woman I had ever seen. Ever. We took each other again and again, saying an unspoken yes each time; experimenting and loving without shame. I knew. We both knew.

And the next morning I had awoken with a start. She wasn't there. I pulled on a pair of shorts and ran topside. She stood on the bow, wind in her auburn hair, looking out on the turquoise sea.

"Janet. Last night. I was going to ask you to marry me."

She turned and there was a seriousness to her lovely face. "Too late, sailor boy."

"What?"

And she had smiled then. "While you were asleep—you don't snore by the way, thank God—while you were asleep, I asked *you*. After all . . . the activity . . . you were your typically stoic self, and so I jerked your head up and down a few times. You said 'Yes,' and you're committed, buster boy. Not exactly a verbal agreement, but I think my lawyers can make it stick in court. You can still carouse and fish and drink with your buddies occasionally. And maybe if I decide to do a film or two in the far future—which I doubt—I still can. But other than those two minor concessions, we've got a contract, you and me. You also agreed to a bunch of babies, a nice little house, and me for your best friend and wife for ever and ever, by the way. How about it, Dusky?"

I had grinned and stuck out my hand. We shook like two businessmen. "Till death do us part, sweet cheeks."

Till death do us part. . . .

And that's the way I awoke now. Janet, dear Janet, was suddenly in my arms, our mouths joined. I was so happy; so happy in my wonderful disbelief. It was she. Really Janet. I felt her lips trace the line of my neck, down my chest to my thighs. I felt the lovely rounded hips, the sharp cones of breast as she went. Her short, close-cropped hair was soft against my stomach. And then . . . then I knew.

"What! Hey!" I sat bolt upright.

The ebony woman lay naked upon me, breasts mashed flat against my thighs, kissing me passionately.

With a sweep of my leg, I knocked her off, onto the floor.

"What in the hell do you think you're doing?"

She looked up at me, her face quivering. "I just thought—"

"Isn't that Senator of yours taking care of you?"

She reached up and touched my arm and started to cry, weeping softly, trembling.

"I'm sorry. I'm so, so sorry. For the last three days I've heard you crying out for her. I've heard you over and over again. And tonight . . . tonight, I just couldn't stand it any longer. I thought that if I tried, if I *did*, and you didn't wake up, that it might help you, captain. And it was good for you; good until you finally woke up. I'm sorry. I just thought . . ."

Her words were lost amid the soft roll of sobs.

I reached up and wiped the sweat off my face. I still had my Rolex. Two o'clock. Morning or afternoon?

"Bimini. That is your name, isn't it?"

She nodded. I pulled her up onto the bed with me, letting her tears stream down my chest. "Bimini, you've been very kind to me. And I appreciate it. You didn't deserve to be treated the way I just treated you. I'm very sorry. But I just couldn't. I can't."

I felt her naked breasts heave against me as she

cried. I felt the damp heat of her thighs on my leg. She pressed herself tightly against me.

"You can't keep holding onto her forever, captain. She's gone."

Bimini lifted her autumn-colored face and looked into my eyes. Gently, she brushed her lips with mine. I felt myself stir. And she felt it, too. She took me in her small hand, stroking me, then kissed me again, her soft tongue searching.

For a moment, one explosive instant, I gave in. My body wanted to. My body wanted her very badly. But I couldn't. Not then, not tomorrow, maybe never. I took both her wrists and pulled her away.

"You are a very beautiful woman, Bimini. There is not a man on earth who wouldn't agree. But it's too soon. I loved her too much."

She sighed a soft, sad sigh.

"I wanted you to have something nice. After all this time, you see, I feel as if I know you. I've cared for you and tended to you, and listened to your awful dreams. In a strange way, I have come to love you. And I just wanted to do this . . . this good thing for you before they came."

"They? For what, Bimini?"

"Captain MacMorgan, in less than an hour, they are coming to carry you out to sea and kill you."

XI

She didn't bother putting her own clothes on before she helped me get dressed. With her she had brought the Navy sweater, the Limey pants and, best of all, my Randall knife.

As she handed it to me, she eyed me steadily, then spoke in her soft West Indies accent:

"Captain, if they find this knife on you, and you do not kill them all, then they will come and kill me. They will know."

I balanced the cold weight of the knife in my hand. Though weak and shaky, I felt better. But strong enough to fight my way out? I didn't know. I decided I couldn't take the chance. I tried to hand the knife back to her.

"Bimini, put this back where you found it. I don't think I'll need it, and I'm not going to take the chance of getting you killed, too. Once on the boat—if I pretend that I am still in a coma—I should be able to

think of something. I should be able to find a way
to escape. But even if I can't, I'm not going to have
us both getting killed."

I was trying to get the last two buttons of my pants
buttoned. My hands wouldn't work right. My fingers
felt as if they had minds of their own. I watched her
step toward me in the soft light of the nearby desk
lamp: tall cocoa-colored beauty with taut proud
body. She pushed the knife away, then pushed my
hands away. Gently, she reached her hands down
into my pants and nimbly did the last two buttons,
and finished by giving me a soft squeeze.

"Why do you fight yourself so, captain?"

"What does that have to do with the knife?"

"I brought the knife for you. I would rather die
than to know there was no one to rescue me from
this terrible place. I will not fight myself, captain.
Not now. Not ever again."

Her face was still flushed from crying, and her
dark eyes were resolute. She pulled herself against
me, hugging me warmly. She was trembling. "You
are a very attractive man, captain. The most attractive
man I have seen in too, too long. Is it wrong of me
to say that I want you?"

"My God, Bimini, they'll be coming before long."

She sighed. "I can see that your body wants me,
too, but . . ."

I pulled her to me, kissed her, touched her breasts
gently, then swung her around and sat her down on
the bed.

"Now listen, you crazy woman!"

She smiled vampishly. "All right, all right! Maybe not now, but someday, sometime, I will have you!"

I rubbed her head good-naturedly. "Maybe. Someday. If I live, goddammit. How many of them will there be? Do you know?"

She reached over and pulled a long, loose-fitting blue cotton dress down over her head. "I'm not sure. The Senator has sent for many men to come. He wants to dismantle much of this place and load it onto boats. He suspects the American government is after him. He has connections in a South American country—I am not sure which one. He is an important man and knows many people. He plans to go there. They have promised him political sanctuary. He wants to take me with him." In a burst of emotion, she clubbed herself on the thigh with a dark fist. "I would die first! I would rather die!"

"His men, Bimini—who are they? Where do they come from?"

She relaxed somewhat and settled back on the bed. "It is as if he has his own small army. Men from Cuba, Haiti, America—many men, black and white. He does things for them; he gets them out of jail or makes it possible for them to come to this country. And once they are in his debt, the Senator makes them work for him. You don't know him, captain. He is a very big man, a very powerful man."

I tried to match the man she told me about with the voice I had heard that night when I put the little bug into the flower vase. A harsh, masculine voice. A bawdy laugh, rich with self-importance.

"How does Ellsworth fit in, Bimini?"

"Ellsworth! Oh, how I hate that man!" Her dark eyes were fierce. "He says things to me—vile things. And when the Senator is not looking, he touches me. Once I slapped him, and he put a knife to my neck. He made me get down on my knees. He enjoyed it. Oh, how that awful man enjoyed forcing me. He made me . . . made me . . ."

"I know what he made you do, Bimini. And the Senator didn't mind?"

"Had I told him, he would have killed Ellsworth—even though Ellsworth runs his drug operation. And then he would have killed me! The Senator, he is so jealous. Yes, he would have certainly killed us both."

"What about Lenze, Bimini? I heard his name mentioned when they thought I was asleep. How does he fit in?"

She paused for a moment, reflecting. "He is the frail little man? Yes? I'm not sure what his position is."

"He supposedly works for the federal government as a special drug investigator."

She tossed her head back and laughed softly. "That little man? He is so frightened of the Senator that he actually jumps when the Senator speaks. If he is with the American government, then the Senator truly has nothing to worry about."

I checked my watch. Two twenty-five. It had to be very early morning. They would not take me out to sea and kill me in the daylight. I got up and went to the door, testing it.

"It's locked," Bimini said. "They always lock me in when I am with you."

"Is there a guard outside?"

"No. You go through that door into the air-conditioner room. There's a big generator, too. It supplies all the power to the island. From there, you walk up the stairs. There's a button to push. You can push a book cabinet away then, and step into the Senator's den."

I went to the desk with the radio equipment shelved on it. I found the VHF and switched to channel 22, the Coast Guard's emergency frequency.

"It's not connected," the woman said. "I tried it this morning when I was beginning to think that you would never wake up again. They must have disconnected it when they put you in here."

I went back to the bed and sat down. My head still hurt, and I was beginning to grow dizzy. She noticed.

"Are you going to be all right? No, no, you're still too ill. I shouldn't have expected . . ."

She was on the verge of tears again. I took her soft hand in mine. "Bimini. You must take the knife. They'll find it." I forced a smile. "I'll pick it up when I come back for you. I promise."

So what do you do when you wait for the footsteps of death to approach? I lay back on the bed, resting. I tried to put myself in their place. Why would they shoot an already comatose man? They wouldn't— unless it was Ellsworth. If it was Ellsworth, he would cut me into little pieces and feed me to the fish. But if it was anyone else, they would probably just weight me down and drop me over.

But where?

If I was to escape from my bonds and surface, and if I was to make it to land, I would have to know.

If. If. *If!*

Perhaps I should take the knife. I might be strong enough to surprise one man, but there would certainly be more than one. It would take two big men to lift me, or three average-sized men.

No, I would have to work the odds. I would have to play the deadly little game. It was my only chance. Besides, they would probably find the knife when they came for me. And then . . . then we would both die.

To ease our nervousness, Bimini began to talk. She talked of her childhood, the little island where she had grown up.

"I was born on a little point of land in the chain of Bahamas called French Wells. My family lived in a little shack there, near the fresh water, across the creek from Crooked Island Veldt, about two hundred and fifty miles south-southeast of Andros."

"I know the place."

"You do!"

"I was at Albert Town once when I was in the Navy. On a liberty, a close friend of mine—he's dead now—a close friend and I went up to Crooked Island for the day. I remember the little white houses in the sun there at Church Grove Landing. What were the people there? Seventh-day Adventists?"

"Yes! The *Grove*! Wasn't it pretty? That's where I grew up."

Oh, it was pretty, all right. Lilliputian houses by the clear tropical sea. Little black children playing in the dirt with the ragged, omnipresent island chickens. White beaches and palm trees, and wonderful fishing. I studied Bimini's lovely face. What was she? Twenty-three, twenty-four? I had been there about ten years before—that would have made her one of the pretty-eyed, shy-faced island girls. Just beginning to blossom; just beginning to feel her womanhood.

"Perhaps we saw each other? Do you think?"

"Perhaps."

"My father worked in the cascarilla-bark groves there. They make medicine and a distaff liqueur from it. I remember that he always smelled so nice. The smell of those islands—wasn't it good? When Columbus came, he named them the fragrant islands. Did you know that, captain?"

I shook my head. "No. I didn't. But I remember the smell. It was a good smell. You still smell of the islands."

She smiled at me. "Do I? I am so glad to hear that. Living here, doing what I do, I feel so . . . so dirty. As if I couldn't possibly smell nice."

I reached out and touched her young face. Bimini: such a pretty name, such a pretty woman. She understood the look in my eye.

She grew serious: "Captain. We still have time. It would not be like with *him*. This would be a small loving thing, and we could make it last until . . . I will make you feel so good, captain. And I know, from the look of you, that you will make me feel better than I have ever felt."

She started to slip the flimsy dress up over her head. I saw the momentary triangle of dark thighs before I took her arms.

"Bimini, no. I told you no, and I mean no."

She sort of shook herself, pouting. "Why must you be so mean? There are so many men that I could have." She snapped her fingers. "Like that! But you! Oh!"

I hugged her, laughing. "Mean? Me? Your friends are coming down here in a few minutes to kill me, and you call *me* mean?"

She drew away from me. "They are not my friends. Do not ever say that again—I hate them!"

"I'm sorry, Bimini. So tell me, then—how did you get involved? How did you come to know the Senator?"

She took a deep breath and sat back. I could tell the subject was distasteful to her. I sat and listened and said nothing.

"When I was a little girl, I grew to hate that pretty little island. I was stupid, as are most children who hate their homelands, and I dreamed of someday escaping. Up on Landrail Point, at the small marina there, they had a wireless radio. When I could sneak away from our little shack, I would go there and listen. I could hear the voices and the music of Miami and Nassau and Havana coming to me, and I dreamed of going to those places.

"Do you remember Landrail Point? Yes? Once a week, the mailboat came there. All the way from Nassau. To me it seemed as if it had come halfway around the world. I made friends with one of the men who ran the boat. He was a fat man, a fat black man, and he said that if I pleasured him, he would take me away. I pleasured him—but I never let him . . . take me." There was a fierce, proud look on her dark face. "I never let any of them take me, ever! Not even the Senator! I knew how to make them feel good, to make them happy, to make it so they didn't care. So he took me to Nassau. Oh, if I had only known what a dirty, nasty place that was! I trained as a nurse. I worked there. One year, two years. I sent most of the money to my mother—my father had died. To make more money I became a dancer in the Ahora Club. A very good dancer. Many rich men wanted me. But the Senator, he was so . . . so convincing. I left with him. I have been with him almost a year now. And I hate him. He has me trapped here; he lets me go nowhere alone. He is so jealous, so afraid that . . . that he won't be the first!"

"I'm surprised he didn't force you."

"Hah! No man on earth could force *me*."

"Ellsworth forced you."

"He took nothing from me. But I should have let him kill me anyway. I know the Senator will kill me if I ever let him take me. That's why I have been with him so long. He hates failure of any kind. And once he succeeds he will dispose of me the way a child rids himself of an old toy. That's why I must escape soon. Before it's too late. Before he takes me too far away from my old home."

I wanted to ask her more questions. I wanted to listen to that fine West Indies voice of hers. She was a strong woman. And she would be a fierce lover. And for some strange reason, she wanted me to be her first. I wondered why. I remembered Vietnam. It was not unusual for the nurses to fall in love and marry a wounded man they had cared for. Perhaps that was it. She had given me my life. And now she wanted to give me hers.

I wanted to ask why, but I couldn't force myself. What terrible instinct of intellect is it that always makes us want to investigate another's motives for wanting to love us?

So instead, I said nothing.

I lay back and closed my eyes, patting her leg tenderly.

And that's when I heard them coming to take me away.

I heard footsteps. And then the click of a deadbolt. And then the door open. And then a voice.

It was the surly, well-modulated voice of Benjamin Ellsworth.

And I knew that I was dead.

XII

"He hasn't woken yet?"

"No. I think he's nearly dead. Poor man."

It was Bimini trying to cover for me. I flinched a little when she called me "poor man." Too much sympathy wouldn't go over well with Ellsworth.

I heard the sound of a match striking, and smelled the monoxide odor of a cigarette.

"He hasn't spoken? Not even a word?"

Bimini's voice was even, professional, unconcerned. I admired her for it.

"He cried out a few times. Let's see, that was . . . yesterday. He mentioned some woman. Janet? Yes. Since then, nothing."

I heard Ellsworth walk toward me; heard the movement of other men behind him. I felt him lean over me: smelled the heat of him, his sour tobacco breath. I had some idea of what he might do. And

he did it. A trick from Vietnam to see if a gook was
really dead.

I felt the radiant glow of the cigarette before it
actually touched my eyelid. I forced myself to relax;
forced my mind to go blank to pain. It hurt. God,
how it hurt. And just when I could take no more,
just when I was about to take a swing at that biblio-
phile face of his, Bimini screamed, "Stop that, you
bastard! Stop it this minute!"

I heard a short scuffle, shook off the urge to join
in, and then:

"You black bitch—if you ever touch me again, I'll
kill you!"

And Bimini hissed at him, biting off each word:
"You ain't man enough to kill me!"

There was a silence, as if Ellsworth was trying to
regain some composure in front of his men. "Bimini,
for your information, this big ugly bastard has already killed at least two, and perhaps more, of the
Senator's people. I was just checking—"

"I don't care who he's killed. And you can kill *him*,
for all I care. But I don't like to see any living thing
mistreated that way. He's dead, can't you see that?
His heart's still beating, but his brain died when you
hit him with that club."

In the silence which followed I heard someone
cough; the shuffle of feet. And then:

"Okay, men. Load him onto that cot. Take him out
to the powerboat. Sammy, you find something heavy.
Some chains, some concrete blocks—it doesn't mat-

ter. And Jones, get some stout rope. I'll want you two to go with me.''

So they carried me up the stairs, through the house, outside. I concentrated on being heavy, limp weight. I wanted them to think of me as something already dead; a big troublesome chunk of meat that they wanted to be rid of.

The two men huffed and puffed as they struggled with me up the stairs and down the loose footing of the shell mound.

''This son of a bitch am some kinda heavy, ain't he, Sammy?''

''Goddam, I guess! Those friggin' shoulders mus' weigh a hundred pounds by themselves! . . . Aw, shit!''

The second one, Sammy, had lost his footing. I felt the stretcher collapse atop him, and I rolled out of it, down the mound, limp as a rag.

I should have made my move then. Just two of them. I wasn't tied. Ellsworth would probably be down at the docks, readying the boat. I should have. But I didn't. I thought about it just a second too long. I wasted that precious second of surprise I needed to take them. What is the saying? He who hesitates . . .

Well, I was lost. No doubt about it. Silently, I swore at myself. Poor man, old wounded killer, seven pounds overweight, and now a second too slow to save his own life.

They were on me in no time.

''Christ, Sammy, watch it, will ya? You like to give me a rupture, droppin' him that way!''

"Well, I didn't mean to, I guaran-goddam-tee you that! I got a bad back as it is. Told the Senator that. Shouldn't be makin' me do this heavy shit."

They grumbled on as they carried me down to the boathouse, their feet clicking and echoing on the wooden dock in the silence of three a.m. They set me down finally, and I could hear the steady wash of water beneath me, and the cracking of pistol shrimp from within their tunicate hideaways on the pilings.

"Okay, get the boat started."

It was Ellsworth.

"You two get him loaded—no, wait a minute. Wrap this canvas around his head. I don't want a trace of him on this boat. And Jones, check him for a weapon—just in case."

I felt big hands pat my legs, thighs, chest, and underarms—a thorough, professional job. I thanked God I hadn't brought the knife. Bimini would have been dead within ten minutes: a soft brown body to join mine in the eternal dark of death and deep water. They dropped me into the boat like a big sack, wrapped my wounded head so that I would not stain the plastic bristle of boat carpet, then, to the roar of twin engines, jetted me toward my final destination.

I kept a map in my mind as we went, sensitive to every shift of direction, every turn, every variation of impact of sea on bow.

I felt us roar northwest, then turn south, probably picking up Big Spanish Channel. I hoped they would stop and get it over with. Why not drop me into the deep water of the pass?

Divers, probably. They were afraid I would be found by the sport divers who hunt the holes and coral heads for Florida lobster. The divers flock to the Keys every August for the sport season.

They were smart. Or Ellsworth was smart. And it was my bad luck. Had they dropped me there, and if I could get loose once underwater, then I knew I could make it back to land.

But offshore? With my battered head and in my dubious physical condition?

I doubted it.

I heard the roar of a passing car, then the echo of our own engines, and I knew I was in trouble. We had just passed under the Bahia Honda bridge, heading for open sea.

How fast were we going? I tried to calculate time and distance. At least forty-five and maybe sixty miles per hour. It was hard to tell. The sleek cruiser knifed through the roll of sea so cleanly that it was difficult to judge speed. But I was familiar with the area, and I knew that if we put more than ten minutes between us and the bridge, I was a goner. An offshore reef line edges the Florida Keys. It runs from five to seven miles out, most of the way up. Once you pass the reef line, the water depth drops off sharply: from twenty feet to more than a hundred feet. In the Navy, my deepest free dive was to 190 feet. A life-and-death plunge one golden dawn in the South China Sea. And 190 feet is not all that great when you consider the free-dive mark set by a fellow Navy diver in 1968: 240 feet—a new American record. I had had nothing wired to my legs back then. And I was in top condition. But at night? With a concussion? Well . . . if they took me over the reef line, I was just as good as dead.

But the odd thing was, I wasn't scared. Death? How can you fear death when life suddenly becomes one absurd succession of breaths and heartbeats which link you to some ghostly otherworld, a world where you used to laugh and love and function with reason? What had I to fear? A few minutes of darkness? The frantic, inevitable attempt to inhale a little life from the nocturnal sea, and then strangulation? If I was going to die, I wanted it that way. I wanted it to be under the water, away from prying eyes and the cold deathwatch of nurses and physicians in the sterile confines of a hospital.

No, I did not fear this death. But I wanted life— life not to *live,* but life to use as a vehicle. A vehicle for revenge. I lay there listening to the damp roar of racing engines, feeling the moist sea wind move across me, and I planned my escape.

"Sammy! Wire him up, Sammy! We're almost there."

Almost there. I did some calculating. We could have come no more than five miles from the Bahia Honda Bridge. That would mean what? Hawks Channel? Yes, Hawks Channel. A deepwater cut between the mainland and the reef. It began narrowly at Key West, then funneled open, wide like a river, skirting the outside archipelago of Florida Keys. I knew how deep the channel was around Key West: from thirty to thirty-five feet. And I knew that it was deeper off Bahia Honda. But how much deeper? Certainly no more than forty-five or fifty feet deep. That wasn't bad. If I could loose myself from my bonds. If I could make it back to the surface. If they didn't hang around to make sure I was down forever. And if I could make the long swim back to shore.

They used wire. Wire and concrete blocks. I could hear the dull impact of cement on cement when Sammy dropped one.

"Jesus Christ, Sammy—are you trying to ruin the Senator's boat?"

"Sorry, Mr. Benjamin, but I got this bad back."

The two flunkies huffed and puffed, rigging me for my last dive.

I was glad it was wire. Some kind of wire cable. It wouldn't bight like good rope. The knots would slip if forced. And I was going to force them. I expanded my chest, my arms, and my legs as much as I could. An old escape artist's trick. A ten-in-one show veteran had showed me how to do it. Julian Ignazio. Let them tighten the rope or wire on the flexed muscles, the inflated chest. And then, when you relaxed, the bonds were already loose enough to work.

"Put most of the weight on his legs. Some on his stomach. That's right—nice and tight. Don't worry about his arms. Mr. MacMorgan will be going nowhere after this."

I almost blessed Ellsworth for those orders. And I hoped they would come back to haunt him.

When they had the weights secured, they dragged me across the carpeted deck to the stern. Low free-board there: I could feel the transom digging into my back. The engines were off now. We were drifting. The sleek glass hull of the powerboat lifted and fell in the slow roll of night sea. Light penetrated my eyelids. Probably a spotlight. Ellsworth wanted to watch me sink away.

"Jones! Hold this a second."

"What're ya gonna do, Mr. Benjamin?"

"I going to make sure this bastard is dead. I know him. He dies hard."

"If you cut him there, Mr. Ben, he's goin' to bleed all over the Senator's—"

"I know what I'm doing, Sammy. Hold him over the transom. Just his head. That's right."

I let my eyes slit open. I could see the dark silhou-ette of Ellsworth coming toward me and the icy glim-mer of the knife. I tested the weights on my legs. I could hardly move them. They had wired me well. A couple hundred pounds or more. Ellsworth came closer and closer. Sammy leaned over me, holding me. A lanky black man with steel in his grip. The other one, Jones, stood back at a distance, as if he didn't care to watch.

So, Ellsworth was going to add a little flourish to my death—his own bloody signature on my throat.

I had to make a move. But I wanted him closer. He had to be closer if I was to have any chance at all. With the weights on my legs, my mobility was nearly zero. I felt his left hand take a tight turn on my hair. I could feel him leaning over me; I could smell his harsh breath. Sammy held me, right hand supporting my head, left hand on my collar.

"Sammy—his eyes. Are his eyes open?"

"Naw. Mr. Ben. Dead people that way sometimes. Eyes slide open. I seen them plenty o' times."

Deep sadistic chuckle.

"Go 'head, Mr. Ben. He all ready for the knife."

I watched the silver blade swing back in its cold arc. And when Ellsworth swung it back at my throat, I was ready. I jammed my thumb in Sammy's ear and shoved his head down to my face. I could feel his thick nose against mine. I felt the blade slice my wrist, then I heard the razor edge grate across the back of Sammy's spine. It had happened too fast for Ellsworth to stop the momentum of his swing.

There was a horrible scream. It was Sammy. He fell sideways onto the deck, holding the back of his neck.

"You kilt me, Mr. Ben! Aw, God! You kilt *me*!"

Ellsworth watched the frenzied movements of the lanky flunky, shocked. Red blood looked black in the harsh white glare of light. Jones rushed up to his friend's side: white puffy face, dazed eyes.

"What are we gonna do, Mr. Benjamin? We got to get Sammy to shore—"

"Shut up!"

"We got to get him back! He's hurt real bad—"

Ellsworth slapped him so quickly with the back of his hand that it surprised even me. And then he leveled his gaze at me. Even in that unsteady light, I saw the hot glow of his hatred for me. The seaman

who had defeated the ROTC hotshot, again and
again and again. I had never seen such a look of
pure hatred. His voice was not even now. It was not
well modulated. It cracked with emotion, like the
voice of an old drunken woman.

"You're dead, MacMorgan. Do you hear me?
You've made one stupid move too many. And now
I'm going to open your throat. Enjoy that breath, *cap-
tain*, because it's your last!"

The blade of the knife caught the light and re-
flected it in bands, back across the face of Ellsworth.
He looked like a madman. And I knew I had but
one chance.

It took a supreme effort from my leg and stomach
muscles; muscles that creaked and cracked with
strain. I kicked the weights on my legs upward while
I fell backward. I felt the blocks of cement peak above
me and then, with a final surrender to gravity, topple
off the stern, dragging me along like a rag doll,
through the black water of Hawks Channel.

How many feet?

I couldn't tell.

It seemed like forever before I finally heard the
soft crunch of weight against coral-sand bottom. I
was at least forty feet down. Forty feet beneath the
night and black sea. The water made a soft familiar
roaring in my ears. I heard the low grunt of some
nearby fish echoing strangely. There was a total void
of light, as if in a dream.

I forced myself to relax. The slightest movement,

the most minuscule effort, burns oxygen. And I could afford no nervous indulgence.

I found the knotted cables. They were banded tightly around my ankles and stomach. Bad knots. Silently, I cursed the bad knots. Any sound knot is relatively easy to untie. But these—these were the messy clusters you see tied by the suburbanite boaters from the north who don't know what in the hell they are doing.

Dangerous knots, because they slip when you don't want them to, and bind when you try to back them out.

I made myself work slowly. Only my hands were alive; my body floated, tethered to the blocks like seaweed, trying to conserve my air. My left wrist ached, as if there were a ten-penny nail driven through it. It was the wrist Ellsworth had cut.

Finally, my left leg was free. But I was running out of air. The cable on my right leg was wrapped and knotted, wrapped and wrapped and knotted again. The knots wouldn't come. I felt myself start to panic; my hands started to pull and strain in a frenzied effort. I was growing dizzy. Steadily, I had been releasing the used air; letting it bubble from my lips when I knew that it was useless to me. But now there was no more air, good or bad, to release.

Once more I ordered myself to work slowly. I had some residual air. You have some residual even when you think there is none left. The first knot was some kind of overhand jumble. I worked it carefully, backing it, loosening it, and finally it came.

One knot left.

How long had I been down? I didn't bother checking my watch. I didn't have time to check it. But it seemed like forever. And forever while working underwater is about three minutes. I once had held my breath for just over six minutes. But that was floating face down in a pretty little resort pool, playing liberty games with fellow SEALS. And when you are relaxed, you can stay down a lot longer.

But I wasn't relaxed now. My air gone, life just one badly tied knot away, I strained to keep my head. I tried slipping the cable down over my foot. No way. Too tight. Once again, I worked at the knot. What if I just tried making it to the top with the blocks on my right leg? Could I haul fifty or more pounds to the top from forty feet of water? Maybe. With plenty of air. And fins. But not now.

My head roared, my chest strained to inhale; motor reflexes taking over. And then my fingers somehow found the way. The knot dissolved beneath them. I reached down with my feet, found the bottom, and pushed off toward the surface. And with the last bit of clear thinking I had left, I let myself float upward and upward, propelling myself gently with easy, even strokes, and finally, just as consciousness was leaving me, I was at the surface, sucking in the good, sweet night air.

The powerboat was still there. Someone scanned the empty sea with the powerful searchlight. They had drifted down and off to my right, back toward Bahia Honda. The light turned toward me. With one more good bite of air, I submerged to about ten feet and swam toward the boat. I saw the light glimmer above me, then pass over. Twenty yards, twenty-five yards, and I found the bottom of the boat above me. I held myself beneath them momentarily, holding myself down, one hand on the glassy hull. Not a barnacle on it. A well-cared-for death craft.

I slid along the bottom toward the bow, careful to cause no noticeable movement beneath the water. Quietly, I surfaced at the sharp thrust of bow and held onto an anchorage eyebolt. I could hear them talking. Sammy moaned softly in the night.

"Jesus Christ, he's gotta be dead by now, Mr. Benjamin! Let's get out of here!"

"We'll go when I say, Jones."

It was the old Ellsworth. Voice controlled, now. He had killed me. He was sure.

"We'll give it a few more minutes."

"But what about Sammy?"

"Sammy's going to be fine. Just fine. I'm going to give you men a little bonus for this. Yes sir, a little bonus."

"Mr. Benjamin, Sammy's my bes' friend, an' I couldn't—"

"You can take the bonus and you will, Jones. I know you men. I know what you're like. You'll take the money whether poor old Sammy dies or not. Isn't that right, Jones?"

Jones muttered something unintelligible. But Ellsworth wasn't listening. He chuckled gaily. "If you only knew how much I wanted that bastard dead. If you only knew. When we get back, I'm going to have a little celebration. Yes sir. . . ."

When the engines rumbled to life, I inhaled deeply and dove toward the bottom. I could stay down now for two or three minutes without difficulty. From beneath the dark water, I heard the vibrant roar of the boat as it jumped up onto plane and headed away, back toward Cuda Key.

When I was sure that it was safe, I surfaced. In the waning moon, drifting westward on the far Key West horizon, I saw the faint glimmer of the disappearing boat. High frost of stars and distant lights off toward Big Pine Key. I checked the back of my left wrist. A deep slice, but no artery had been damaged. I floated for a few minutes, relaxing on the bleak night sea, then started my swim back to shore, back toward Ellsworth and Cuda Key, soft roll of ocean behind me.

XIII

Stormin' Norman Fizer came to pay my bill and check me out of the Key West Naval Hospital. He came at midnight on a Sunday night—less chance of us being seen. I heard the echo of his long heavy steps well before he got to my private room. He was all wry smiles and congratulations: the consummate CIA man in his obligatory three-piece suit.

"You look strangely exotic in that white turban, Dusky."

"Much thanks, sahib. And what the hell took you so long?"

He sat on the corner of the high hospital bed while I pulled on pants and socks and my Top-Siders.

"I just wanted to make sure you are all right. Had a little talk with the doctors."

"And they told you exactly what I told you over the phone. CAT scan negative. Spinal tap negative. A mild concussion and, aside from a slight indentation in my skull, I'm A-okay. Right?"

He laughed. "Right. So I didn't believe you. Sue me. I just knew how anxious you were to get out of this place, and I wanted to be sure. You did a good job for us—we want to make sure you get the best of care. I saw you that day, remember? And I admit that I find it a little hard to believe you're being released so soon. You were a mess, captain. Some kind of mess."

I was a mess, all right. Never had a three-mile swim seemed like such an eternity. The tide kept slipping me westward. My left wrist ached, and my damaged brain kept playing tricks on me. It seemed as if I was getting farther and farther away from land, and then I imagined bottle-nosed dolphins rising to talk with me. Maybe they did talk, I don't know. They told me to relax; to let myself relax and sink and join them. Far Orion, slipping down on the western horizon, became Key West, and the lights of Big Pine Key became a distant constellation. Everything was a gauzy haze of unreality, and all I wanted to do was sleep. Go to sleep and join the sleek hunters—my friends, the dolphins.

It was a tittering, bronze dawn when my feet finally touched bottom off Sugarloaf Key. The early tourist fishermen roared along Highway A1A, hauling gaudy weekender boats behind their cars. I wondered what I looked like to them. Neptune climbing from the sea? Or just one more Florida Keys wino trying to recover from a Homeric hangover with an early-morning swim?

The wino, of course. Just one more down-and-out wino.

They didn't stop. No one stopped for the sagging, damaged man, and that was good. I didn't want them to stop. In Ellsworth's mind, I was dead. And I wanted no one to know otherwise. So I struggled down the edge of the road to an all-night 7-Eleven store, called Stormin' Norman from a pay phone, bullied an operator into connecting us, dime or no dime, and then settled back to sleep in the fresh morning heat when I knew that he was on his way.

I was a mess, all right.

I dreamed gibberish and, when Fizer arrived, my tongue wasn't in any mood to take commands.

"Dusky. Dusky! Jesus Christ, buddy, what did those guys do to you?"

"Arrrg . . . numbf . . ."

"Hang on, buddy. I'm going to call an ambulance."

"No!"

Bad as I was, I wanted no part of an ambulance. The fewer people who knew, the better. I wanted to enjoy the anonymity only death allows. I wanted to enjoy it up until the time I had my hands around Ellsworth's throat.

So, reluctantly, Stormin' Norman had driven me to the naval hospital. He made all the arrangements: private room, military doctors and nurses; people with high security clearance. They worked to make me live while perpetrating news of my death.

And after a few days, and after a huge bank of

tests, the doctors, shaking their heads in curious disbelief, agreed that I was fit to go.

"So where are you going to stay?" Fizer asked as he watched me dress.

"I've got some friends on Cow Key. Good people. Man and a wife and a teenage daughter. I think they'll help me out. And I can trust them."

Stormin' Norman cleared his throat and toyed with his wedding band nervously.

"Like I said, Dusky, you did a good job for us. Damn good job. That caretaker's finding the drugged dogs wasn't your fault. It was a difficult mission, and you had to play the odds."

I pulled a clean black Key West Conchs T-shirt tenderly over my head and tucked it in. "Wait a minute, Norm. You're not about to say what I think you're going to say?"

He motioned for me to sit down. "What I'm getting at is this. They found all but one of your bugs. Putting one in the sauna bath was a real stroke of genius, by the way. We've got all the information we need. The Senator is going to spread the word among his political buddies that, on Friday night, he's going on a big fishing trip to the Dry Tortugas. In that big two-hundred-thousand-dollar sportfisherman of his. Only he's not going to make it. The boat's going to burn and sink."

"*Right.*"

Norm smiled. "You catch on quick. He's going to rig his own death. Kill some of his own people, dress one to look like him, then take a seaplane to some as yet undisclosed South American country. He knows we're on to him."

"So what's your move?"

"On Thursday we're going to arrest our own Mr. Lenze. We've got him good: falsified reports, et cetera. And we're going to put him away for a long, long time."

"And what about the Senator and Ellsworth?"

Fizer cleared his throat. "The Senator needs more rope yet. We're talking about an extremely powerful man here, Dusky. We're going to let him go to South America. We're going to let him hang himself. And then we'll go after extradition papers. We'll use all the political clout the American government has."

"Which isn't all that much, thanks to a certain wishy-washy Pres—"

"I *know* that, Dusky! Goddammit, don't you have any faith in me after Cambodia? I'm not one of their flunkies. I have the job I have because I'm good at it. Damn good at it. I'm telling you we'll get him. And we will. It may take a year or two."

"And what about Ellsworth?"

Stormin' Norman sighed a heavy sigh. One more military man who, I could tell, hated the political bureaucracy as much as I. But he dealt with it; dealt with it because that was the way it had to be done. And if he didn't do it . . . well, America, land of the free, home of the brave, and harbor of the bureaucratic noblemen; the political upper class that rules us and uses our money as if we were the fools of serfdom. And in many ways, we are fools: fools to let them; to let them ravage our forests and rivers, arm and arm with big business; fools to let them condemn to slavery the poor blacks and Indians and Hispanics through their plush welfare programs which would rob any race, any people, of the most inalienable of all rights—human initiative.

"We've got to let Ellsworth go, too, Dusky. He'll be on the boat."

"He killed my wife, my kids, my best friend, goddammit!"

"He's the rope, Dusky. He's the rope that's going to hang the Senator. And even if we tried to arrest him, we probably couldn't make it stick. Attempted murder—maybe. If you got the right judge, the right jury, the right lawyer. But that's small potatoes."

I rubbed my face with my hands. I wiggled my wrist. It was feeling better. A deep cut, down to the bone, but I could still use it, once the stitches were out. I wondered what had happened to Sammy. Dead, probably.

"So you're telling me that I'm out of the picture, right, Norman?"

"In your present physical condition? Yes."

"I feel fine!"

"And you look like hell. Don't feed me that 'I feel fine' crap. You're not fit, Dusky. The gang-war ploy is out. I'm not going to be responsible for your death."

"You won't have to."

He looked at me in open appraisal. "We won't allow a slaughter, Dusky. Good people or bad, we won't allow it. If you were fit, we would want certain things destroyed. A boat or two, part of the house—just enough chaos to force them into trying to rescue the important papers, the big money stash—the stuff we need to find to nail them in court."

"And if I was fit, and if I did try it and a few people got in my way, then what?"

Fizer shook his head wearily. "I can't believe I'm going along with this conversation."

"But what if?"

"*If* you tried it—which you won't because I can't allow it—if you tried it, it would be strictly hands off the Senator. A couple of local drug runners get killed, and it barely makes the inside page of the Miami *Herald*. But if a Senator gets killed in a drug-gang war, the world press will come here on the run. Big federal investigation, Senate hearings—and we don't need that kind of publicity. There's been too much of it as it is."

"Okay, Norm, I'm too sick for the mission. Case closed, okay?"

He snorted sarcastically. "Right. Sure, Mac-Morgan." And then he allowed a narrow smile to cross his face. "Do you think you're too sick to give me a full report?"

So I told him all about Cuda Key. I told him about the layout of the island, the layout of the house, and I told him about the woman, Bimini—minus a few of the more private details.

"She really did save my life, Norm. And she

helped me effect my escape. She's trapped there. Kind of a well-paid prisoner. So if you do close in on them, go easy on her. I owe her a lot."

Fizer snickered. "Why is it all the dames go for you, MacMorgan? God, even over in Nam."

"Must be my boyish charm," I said. Fizer caught the sourness in my voice.

"Sorry, Dusky. I was out of line there. She was some woman, your wife. I'm sorry."

By the time I had finished my report, answering and reanswering Fizer's questions, we were at my friend Hervey Yarbrough's house on Cow Key. A little plank-and-tin shanty at the water's edge, yard cluttered with old boat hulls and crab traps; the typical household retreat of the native Floridian all caught in the sweep of headlights.

Slowly I climbed out of the car and looked back in. "Good luck, Norm. I hope you get them all. And if you can, smack that bastard Lenze for me."

I expected the familiar chuckle, but it never came. In the soft glow of the car's dome light, I saw an honest concern in the dark, tough eyes of my friend.

"And good luck to you, Captain MacMorgan. I hope we can work together again sometime."

"We will, Norm. We will."

As the car roared away down the dirt-and-shell road, Hervey's big Chesapeake Bay retriever came charging out at me. I remembered what the caretaker on Cuda Key had said about Chesapeakes and I laughed softly—but not before first calling the dog's name out to let him know that I was a friend. He trotted up fearlessly, short curl of hair bristling, sniffed me, recognized me, then trotted heavily away, wonderfully arrogant. I might be a friend of the family, but I was no friend of his. He would tolerate my presence, but I should expect no tail-wagging foolishness from him. Strictly a one-family dog, to the death.

At the Chesapeake's warning, lights in the Yarbrough residence started blinking on. The front screen door swung open, and I could see Hervey's bulky silhouette, shotgun in his hand, trying to peer through the darkness.

"Whoever's out there better have a dang good excuse!"

"It's me, Hervey. Dusky MacMorgan."

Hervey took two steps backward, sort of sagged, and dropped the gun. "Great God a'mighty . . . is that really you, Dusky?"

I walked toward the house. "Yeah, it's me, Hervey. What in the world is wrong with you?"

I could see his face by that time. His eyes were wide and round as if he were about to have a heart attack.

"Hey, Hervey! What's the matter?"

He studied me for a moment. "You *are* alive! You ain't no ghost!" He backed away and finally plopped down in an old chair. And then he started laughing. Laughing like a maniac; laughing until the tears rolled. Mrs. Yarbrough and their teenage daughter were up by that time. They looked at Hervey, then looked at me, and then they started roaring too.

"What in the world is going on here?" I demanded. "I just stopped in to ask—"

"We thought you was dead!" the woman howled, her shoulders and heavy breasts shaking beneath her nightgown. "The ol' man there thought you was a *ghost!*"

I started to ask for an explanation, but before I could, the daughter, shy in her soft blue nightshirt, brought me the front page of a newspaper. It was the Key West *Citizen.*

"Charter Captain Missing, Now Presumed Dead."

The story which followed quoted unnamed federal authorities, detailed my life in Key West, mentioned the recent deaths of Janet and Ernest and Honor.

So that was it. A plant. A newspaper plant from one Stormin' Norman Fizer. He had known what I was going to do all along. His pleas for me to give up the mission, to turn it back over to them, had all been a ruse. He wanted me to make the decision, and he wanted me to make it on my own—but he was obviously planning on me to go ahead with it.

I too started to chuckle. And then laugh. And then roar, in long sweeping bursts. It felt good to be with that family, in the warm confines of a solid home base, laughing among friends. It was the first time I had laughed in a very long time, and, momentarily, I felt the hatred and the thirst for revenge drain out of me.

The teenage daughter, April, was the first to recover. She came to me, touched the bandage on my head tenderly. "Daddy, now stop that laughin', hear me? Cap'n MacMorgan here has been hurt. We got to take care of him."

Hervey and his wife sobered momentarily, but the craziness of it all got to them again.

"A *ghost*! Hahahahahahahaha. . . ."

The two of them sagged back in their chairs helplessly.

The girl turned to me. "You got to forgive them, cap'n. My momma and daddy is crazy as loons when the spell's on them. *Daddy, quit that laughin'!*"

"A *ghost!* Hahahahahahahaha. . . ."

She smiled at me in embarrassment. "Well, can I get somethin' for you to eat? We got some beans and fish in the icebox. Won't take me a minute to heat it."

I stood up shakily. "No, I'm not hungry, little one. A little sleepy, maybe. But not hungry."

She took me by the elbow and started to steer me toward the bedroom; a short, raven-haired teenager, pretty plain face with heavy thrust of country-girl breasts beneath the blue nightshirt. "You take my bed, cap'n. Sheets are clean. You sleep in my bed tonight."

"No, no, little one, just give me a pillow and I'll take the couch."

"You're a guest in our house, an' we won't have no guest sleepin' on the couch. You can talk to Momma and Daddy in the mornin'. But now you need sleep. Your eyes tell me as much."

"Now listen to me, little one," I started to protest, but she cut me off.

"I won't hear another word about it—an' quit callin' me 'little one.' It was okay a few years ago, but now I'm a grow'd woman, cap'n. I'm eighteen years old an' I won't have it."

"Then call me Dusky."

"Okay, I'm April, an' you're Dusky, and now Dusky is gonna lay back an' go to sleep in April's bed."

I think I was still fronting shaky arguments when my head hit the pillow and I collapsed into sleep. . . .

I spent the next few days getting my strength back and eating like a horse. I wanted rare steaks and black beans, Cuban bread, and I even managed a beer or two. I might not be at my best, but I would be strong enough when I made my second visit to Cuda Key.

The morning after my arrival, I had walked out into the yard with Hervey, his little corner of secluded estate alive with the cackle of scruffy chickens, the lumbering Chesapeake, and August sun.

"I've got a favor to ask of you and your family, Hervey."

But he was way ahead of me. He carefully opened a fresh foil packet of Red Man chewing tobacco and stuck a big wad of it in his mouth. "You don' have to worry, Dusky. My ol' lady or the girl won't say nothin' to nobody 'bout your stayin' here. Me neither, o'course. You got your reasons, an' I don't care what they are. I trust you. An' tha's enough."

So I stayed. I pressed money on them to buy the groceries I wanted, and they accepted reluctantly. I knew about the Yarbroughs and I knew of their pride. A strange thing about them, and native Floridians like them: they could have sold their corner of waterfront jungle for well over a million dollars; money enough to see them moved through two generations. And they could have sat back in their new Cadillacs or looked on from the confines of their new concrete-and-plastic houses and watched the big-business builders rip the old wooden house down and replace it with a multistory concrete block of condominiums that would have housed three hundred Northerners. But what is a million dollars when it means watching your life and your heritage being ripped out by the roots? Too many Floridians made that dismal error. But not the proud ones, the strong ones; not people like the Yarbroughs. They would rather have their homes and their happy poverty.

So I stayed. And they finally took my money— after I said I would find another hiding place if they didn't.

By Thursday I was feeling good. Really good. Bright multicolored halos no longer surrounded lights, and April had removed the stitches from my wrist with tender concentration. To test myself I jogged a mile up the road to Stock Island, then ran back at about half speed. I timed myself with the Rolex. Nine minutes up, six and a half minutes back. Not bad. On the Yarbroughs' lawn was a big lazy oak tree, draped with Spanish moss. I picked out a sturdy limb, jumped up and grabbed it, and then did twenty-nine good pull-ups. When I was in shape, really in shape, I could do thirty-eight. But twenty-nine was about twenty-two more than your average American male can do, and I was satisfied. I pushed myself through about fifteen minutes of good stretching exercises, and when I was through huffing and puffing in the hot noonday sun, I turned to see April watching me. She wore short cut-off jeans and a blue man's shirt, the tails tied beneath her breasts and above her flat stomach. She looked at me with frank disapproval, her long black hair swinging back across her buttocks as she turned away in some sort of strange protest.

"April! Hey!"

I hurried to catch up with her. When I caught her, I took her elbow and swung her gently around. "What's wrong, April? Huh? Why were you looking at me like that?"

Her pretty face was obviously red from anger, and I realized for the first time that she had amber—almost golden—brown eyes.

"What's wrong? Men!" she half-shouted in disgust.

She started to stalk off again, but I stopped her.

"Hey! Just give me a hint." I tried a smile. "Was it something I said?"

She glowered at me and, somehow, it made her look older. Pretty little girl; I had known her since she was just a barefooted kid, playing in the dirt. The pretty little daughter of a friend, and now I felt odd seeing her as a woman for the first time.

"You wanna know what's wrong with me, Mr. Dusky MacMorgan? Well, I'll tell you. I spent the best part of th' last four days worryin' myself sick about whether you'd get well or not. You tol' Daddy what had happened, an' maybe you tol' Momma. I don' know—figured it wasn't none o' my business. Didn't ask you the first question. Jus' wanted you ta get well, tha's all. But then I walk out here to feed the chickens an' I see you runnin' around an' swingin' from the trees like a big blond ape—like you're tryin' to kill yourself for sure, an' . . . an' . . .'' Her face flushed even more, close to tears. ''An' it jus' made me mad! Oh . . . men!'' She whirled around and stomped off, oblivious to my stammered explanations.

So what do you do? What could I do? I went inside the house, showered, fried myself a steak, and opened a beer. I had somehow hurt her feelings by, in her mind, hurting myself. I was touched by her concern. And I wanted to explain to her: explain why I had to push my recovery; explain why people over thirty sometimes fail to notice the inexorable transition to maturity in people they have known only as children. I wanted to talk to her, adult to adult, but she wasn't back by two p.m. And I had to head up to Boca Chica for a little meeting with D. Harold Westervelt.

The colonel was swimming his laps when I arrived. He opened the front door of his neat suburban home dripping wet, a towel draped around his neck. He seemed pleased to see me—but not pleased enough to cut short his workout.

''I must apologize,'' he explained as we walked

back to the patio, "but I believe that even the smallest concession to one's discipline inevitably leads to another concession, and then another and another." He laughed shortly. "I'm afraid my penchant for discipline used to drive my poor late wife crazy. But I'm fixed in my ways, and I can't afford to let myself change now, captain. I swim half a mile in the morning: six a.m. winter or summer, rain or shine, seven days a week. I work until the early afternoon, lunch on tossed salad, then swim another half a mile and do my calisthenics. So you'll have to excuse me for another twenty minutes or so."

So I sat on a plastic lawn chair with my honey and tea and watched the colonel. His pool was unlike most backyard pools. It was about twenty-five yards long and only, perhaps, ten yards wide—built for exercise, not patio parties. He swam with long, strong strokes. His shaved head cut through the water like the bow of a boat, and his broad shoulder muscles knotted and extended as he went. At fifty-some years of age, Colonel D. Harold Westervelt was an amazing physical specimen. In fact, he was an amazing physical specimen compared to most men at any age.

When he was finished with his laps, he jumped out of the pool, toweled off briefly, did seventy-five push-ups, rested momentarily, then did a hundred sit-ups, using the towel beneath his hips as a pad. His calisthenics finished, he rinsed off in the pool, dried himself, pulled on black warm-up pants and jersey, then sat beside me on the patio. He wasn't even breathing hard.

"I appreciate your patience, captain. Few people would understand."

"A very impressive display, colonel."

"It wasn't meant to be impressive, only functional." He turned his icy blue eyes toward me. D. Harold Westervelt was one tough cookie. And I was glad I was on his side.

He stood up. "I've read your report. You did well, captain. Very well." He eyed me for a moment, going over me from head to toe, the way someone might study a car they are considering for purchase. "You've lost the excess weight, I see. What are you, about two-oh-five?"

"I'm not sure now, colonel. But around two-ten when I'm right. Few people guess it as closely as you did. They usually guess a lot heavier."

"The shoulders throw them off. If the rest of your body were in proportion to your shoulders, you'd weigh . . . what? Fifty or sixty pounds more?"

I smiled. He didn't smile back. He was all business, that man. How long had I known him? Well, a long, long time; friends through mutual interests and a military past. And still I was never given even the first indication that he was somehow involved with Norm Fizer's agency. And I probably would never have known had it not been for . . .

"I assume you are here because you want to reinvolve yourself with that Cuda Key business?" he said, breaking in on my thoughts.

"That's correct."

"I suggest you move out this evening."

"That was my plan."

"And weapons?"

"That's why I'm here. I'm afraid I lost the dart pistol. And my knife. But I plan to get them back."

"Follow me," D. Harold Westervelt said. And he led me back to his laboratory and armament room and unlocked the steel fire door. Once inside, I took a seat.

"How are you feeling now, captain?" He looked meaningfully at the head bandage I still wore.

"Fit. Ready."

He nodded. "Good. Never underestimate your abilities, and never overestimate your strengths. They can be fatal errors." He pulled open the floor safe, reached in, and retrieved another Webber dart pistol. "I think we discussed before the problems of peace-time warfare? Because of that, I will give you only one dart loaded with the scorpionfish toxin. Let us say . . . the third dart—which you can change, of course. The others will contain a powerful knockout drug, similar to that which you used on the dogs."

"And if I use this drug on the dogs?"

Colonel Westervelt shrugged. "It may kill them, but probably not. It depends on their size. It will knock out a hundred-and-sixty-pound man for two, maybe three hours. If you use it on the dogs, they will give you no problem for some time."

He closed the floor safe, covered it via the button on the wall, then unlocked one of the many gun cabinets. From a top shelf he produced a small mahogany box. He put the box on the table before me and opened it. Inside, in neat rows, were small metal caps tipped with some kind of hard black rubber.

"I made these myself. They've been well tested, believe me."

"Tips for the Cobra arrows?"

He nodded. "Actually, they give the expert bowman the two ideal options. Shoot an adversary in the head at a range of up to a hundred yards and you will knock him cold. Hit him on the left side of his chest, or in the throat, and you will kill him. In this box you will also find the regular lead weights which you must add to your shafts for perfect balance. These tips require only one each. Now, if you were to attach, say, a thermite grenade—"

"I have no grenades, colonel."

"You will, Captain MacMorgan. You will."

XIV

I would spare as many as I could; spare the leaching, drugged-up flunkies that the Senator held under his spell. But the ones who got in my way were dead. Just as Ellsworth was dead. He was a corpse and didn't even know it.

Hervey Yarbrough brought the *Sniper* around for me. It could have been a touchy situation, because when you care for a boat, really care for it, you want no one's hands on the controls but your own. And even though I said nothing about my concern, Hervey understood.

"Dusky, I want you to know you ain't got nothin' to worry about. I'll bring that pretty boat of yours up here jes' careful and sweet as can be. Treat her like she was my own."

"I know that, Hervey. Does it show that much?"

"Naw, but I know how I feel—the idea of somebody else runnin' my boat jes' kinda makes my stomach roll. As my daddy said: 'Boy, there's three things in this life you should never loan: your boat, your dog, and your wife.' "

"In that order, Hervey?"

He grinned a big toothy grin at me. "If it ain't, it's dang close."

The *Sniper* made the cut into the narrow Cow Key Channel right at sunset. I hadn't seen her in too, too long, and the sight of her, looking black in the golden angle of sunlight, riding high and sleek across the turquoise slick of horizon, put a lump in my throat. I knew then how the knights of old must have felt when their squires brought their energized, armored war horses to them. The *Sniper* was ready. And so was I.

Hervey brought her in with the expertise only a lifetime on the sea affords; an eggshell landing, the engines pulled into reverse without any clatter of gears to stop her sternway. Once we had fixed lines and spring lines and had her properly bumpered, I went over my gear and stowed it all in the watertight knapsack I would carry.

"I did jes' like you said," Hervey told me as we stood in the new dusk, side by side, at his rickety wooden dock. "I tol' the folks at the marina that the . . . the . . ."

"The executor of my will?"

"Yeah. I tol' them he had as't me to haul her out and go over her before gettin' an appraisal for your estate."

"Good."

"They was all real sad about your death." He chuckled softly in the darkness. "Almost got a little teary-eyed myself listenin' to 'em talk. To hear them tell it, you was half Boy Scout, half God, an' half fish hawk."

"All the recent dead are, Hervey. It's too bad we can't appreciate people while they're still alive. Huh?"

"Tha's the dang truth, Dusky. The dang truth. Makes me want to go inside an' give tha' girl of mine an' the ol' woman a big hug. This life does have a way o' slippin' right through our fingers, don't it?"

"Yes. Yes, it does."

Hervey cleared his throat and, with well-practiced fingers, took a fresh chew of tobacco from the Red Man pouch. "I got a feelin', cap'n, that what you got planned tonight might be a little on the dangerous side."

"A little."

He spat calmly into the dark water. "May not look like it, but in my day I was some kinda rough when it come to a fight. Figure I'm still he-coon enough to take care of three or four of them dopeheaded bastards if push come to shove."

It was an eloquent offer, honestly made. If I wanted help, Hervey Yarbrough was willing and ready. I put my hand on his thick shoulder.

"I appreciate it, Hervey, but I've got to do this alone. I've been trouble enough as it is."

He spat again. "Ain't been no trouble, far as I can

see. Well, you'll be wantin' to get a little shut-eye before you shove off, huh?"

"I think I'd better."

I went into April's room and shut the door. I hadn't seen her since that afternoon. I didn't want to leave without saying goodbye and thanking all three of them, but—well, any farewell might imply that I might never come back. And I didn't want them saddled with any additional worry. So, at midnight, goodbyes or not, I would just slip away.

I turned on her desk lamp. A small clean room adorned with the things common to the rooms of teenage girls everywhere: high school pennants, Polaroid snapshots, and little bottles of department-store perfume. Snoop that I am, I went through the photographs; stop-action capsules of a single human life in gentle flight. The little girl, the tomboy, the new teenager banking toward womanhood. I noticed something odd: no boys in the photographs with her. And she was a pretty girl: breasts and ripe young body built for love. I wondered about the curious absence of the obligatory adoring male. She was no lesbian—the way she shyly flirted told me that. She was all young woman, strong and sure—and maybe that was it. You see it sometimes in the independent ones, the best of the females—they can't find a male strong enough to accept them, to complement them. I put the photographs back the way I had found them, amused with the new puzzle of April Yarbrough, the young woman I had known before only as a little girl.

There was a mirror over her dresser. Carefully, I unwound the head bandage and, with the aid of a cheap little hand mirror, took a look at the back of my head. The blond hair was yellow and then rust-colored where Ellsworth had clubbed me. I touched the spot tenderly.

"Damn!"

It still hurt. No doubt about that. But it was too late to worry about. And too unimportant.

I awoke when I heard the bedroom door open. All was darkness: not a light on in the house. I heard the tick-tock-ticking of the grandfather clock in the living room.

Still half asleep, I reached mechanically for my Randall knife. In Vietnam I had kept it under my pillow. Always. In my dream, that's where I was— back in Nam where a moment's hesitation could kill you just deader than hell. The knife wasn't there, of course. It was back on Cuda Key. And by the time I realized it, the approaching figure was upon me, beside the bed. I reached out, grabbed an arm, swung the adversary around, and pulled the body down on me, taking a strong cross-chest hold on it—and felt the firm heave of breasts.

"April!"

"Jesus Christ, man! You always wake up this way?"

I fumbled for the little desk lamp beside the bed and switched it on. She wore the same soft blue nightshirt she had worn the first night I arrived, and now it was hiked up above her bikini panties in disarray. She brushed stray ropen hair back over her shoulders, unconcerned with exposed tan legs and the dark bulge of hips.

"What are you—"

"Came to say goodbye, that's what! Lordy, you liked to mash me flat, the way you grabbed me!"

I settled back while she sat on the edge of the bed. I smiled and looked at her meaningfully. "Not much danger of that," I said.

She blushed and slapped at me. "Well . . . at least you noticed. There for a while I thought all you saw when you looked at me was that barefooted little girl."

"April, I'm sorry about this afternoon. I should have explained things to you. You have a right to know."

So I told her. I told her everything, leaving out only names and my new involvement with Fizer's agency. And as she listened, I saw her face soften and the moisture fill her golden eyes.

"And that's it," I finished. "And if you start getting weepy on me, I'll turn you over my knee. You're old enough to accept the fact that some people are just plain evil. But I'm going to get them. Every one of them."

She looked away from me momentarily, gathering her composure, then turned back.

"You shoulda tol' me earlier," she said.

"Had I known my rush to recovery was going to upset you, I would have."

Her eye widened in brief anger. "It's not jus' that! Can't ya' see I . . . I . . . I *care* about you?"

She turned away, and I knew that she was crying now. Gently, I pulled her head down to my chest: warm raven hair, scented with perfume. I stroked her head and spoke softly. "April, if there was ever to be another woman, I would want her to be just like you. But you're too young, sweetheart. You have too much—"

"Too young!" She bolted upright, out of my arms. "Are ya blind or what? I'm a woman now, Dusky MacMorgan! Eighteen or forty-eight—a woman's a woman. An' all I'm wantin' now is a strong man and a bunch 'a strong babies, an' . . ."

She stared deep into my eyes, and I saw her face change; feeling, as I did, my own body come alive with the scent of her, the nearness of her, the love in her. April leaned down and kissed me softly. The sexuality in the kiss was as strong and tangible as summer musk. Her lips were hot and swollen, and I pulled her down on me, felt her legs and hips swing up, onto the bed, and press against my body, naked beneath the sheet. She trembled beneath my arms, her mouth open and wanting as I slid my hand gently up the undulations of stomach and ribs to the firmness of young, heavy breasts.

"Dusky, oh Dusky, I've wanted ta kiss you like this so bad. . . ."

It was all there, everything I could ever want to make my return to the world of the living. A good woman, a strong woman; an eighteen-year-old woman so aware of her wants that she had no time for coyness. I considered it. I really did. For a long, passionate minute, I knew that I could do no better than this April Yarbrough. But I wasn't ready to rejoin the living; not yet. What had I to offer her save a night of passion and whispered words of love? In a few more hours I would be on Cuda Key, and I could afford no attachments, no woman to live for, no love to inspire within me a fear of death.

I pulled her face down onto my shoulder, kissed her gently on the cheek and whispered, "April, I want you. You know that. But not now, not tomorrow, and not the next day. Now listen to me! I want you to experience a little of life first. Date. Have fun. Go off to college. And then . . . if you're still interested in a scarred-up old man, well . . ."

She sat up. I expected her to cry. But she didn't. She brushed the hair away from my face, letting her hand linger on my cheek, and then she smiled. "Whew! Look at me, will you—the first man I didn't want to fight off, an' he turns *me* down."

She began to laugh softly; a good laugh. I took her hand. "You understand, don't you?"

She nodded. "I do. An' I'm gonna hold you to what you said." She allowed herself another chuckle, this time bashful. "An', from the feel of you, you're sure fire breeding stock—no doubt about that."

I laughed with her; innocent, bawdy, bedroom laughter. And then I hugged her tenderly, fought to keep control of my own body, and allowed myself one last kiss.

"You're leavin' tonight, aren't you, Dusky?"

"That's right, April."

"Well, I ain't the type to try an' stop a man from doin' what he has to do. So I'll wish you luck. An' make you promise you'll come back to see me sometime."

"I'll do that, April. Promise."

She smiled a girlish smile at me. "Couldn't use some help, could ya? I'm small but strong. We're part Indian, ya know."

I smacked her on the rump. "No! And get out of here before I change my mind."

And then she was gone: purposeful wiggle of pantied hips, vampish flash of perfect breasts from beneath the blue nightshirt, and soft laughter as she disappeared down the hallway.

I sighed heavily and lay back on her pillow. The room was still scented with her. Any attempt to sleep, I knew, would be useless. Goodbye, April Yarbrough. I hope we meet again. When you are ready, and when I am ready. Soon.

I gave it a few minutes, hardening myself for my upcoming mission, refreshing the memories within me that would bring to surface the stoic anger I would need to succeed.

It didn't take much effort.

By my Rolex, it was nearly midnight. I climbed out of bed, did ten minutes of stretching exercises, then dressed. Black sweater, dark British commando pants, black watch cap. The cap was tight on my head, and it hurt momentarily.

Outside, the wind had freshened; heavy, late-August storm wind, thunderheads bruised and anvil-shaped in the flare of distant lightning. I walked out of the house, across the dirt yard, down to the dock. Someone was standing there, hands on hips, watching the approaching storm.

It was Hervey.

"Looks like you're in for some weather, cap'n," he said when he heard my footfall.

"Southeast wind. Probably swing around and hit out of the northwest."

"Yep."

The *Sniper* strained and rolled against her lines like a nervous horse. There was another flash of lightning, a distant rumble, and I could see green pustules of feathering waves on the open sea. The damp storm wind roared and receded in the high palm trees and leached a strange ozone and protein odor from the water.

"I didn't even hear you get up, Hervey."

"Well, you was sorta busy at the time."

"Oh."

So he knew. And what can you say to a friend who knows you were with his daughter?

"She's a good girl, Hervey. It wasn't what you might think."

He chuckled quietly and produced his Red Man. "Chew?"

"Don't mind if I do."

I took the moist leaves, rolled them, and pushed the wad back into my cheek, feeling the sweet taste move across my tongue.

"Funny thing," Hervey said. "You raise a young'un an', after a time, you stop seein' them grow. April there has always been jes' a little girl ta me. Guess I was blin' not to see that she'd growed into a woman."

"A good woman, Hervey."

"No doubt 'bout that. Always been kinda different, that one. Not like the other young'uns ya see gallivantin' around in cars an' drinkin' wild an' such. Like she was born old or somethin'. An' probably too smart for her own good—straight A's in school an' never really had to work at it."

"Hervey . . ."

He turned to me and smiled; a strange, sad smile. "You got nothin' to apologize to me for, Dusky. If nothin' happened between you an' April, that's fine. An' if somethin' did, well, it's business 'tween you an' her. Sorta hope it did, really. Girl's first time oughta be nice."

"I wish I could have, Hervey. But I couldn't."

"Well, 'least you finally seed how tha' pretty little thing feels 'bout you. Obvious ta me an' the ol' woman all along. We was wonderin' if you was blin' or somethin'. You lost you one good woman, Dusky. And ya need another—not a woman to replace her; jes' a different one. A woman to he'p ya get goin' again. To give ya some babies and he'p ya make it

through the resta your life. No shame in needin'—
when you're ready. An' when tha' time comes . . .
well, I'd be proud to let you court my daughter." He
shook his head and chuckled again. "God knows, she
needs a strong man. She's some kinda hell on wheels,
tha' girl. I can't handle her; ain't smart enough or
strong enough. I ain't ashamed to admit it, neither."

I slapped him gently on the back. "And I would
be proud to date April, Hervey. And I might show
up at your doorstep some evening. But I'm not ready
yet. And neither is she—and she understands that."

We both stood silent for a few minutes, feeling the
warm blow of storm in our faces. Finally, Hervey
said, "Got some hot coffee up ta the house. Let me
put some in a thermos for ya. You're gonna need it."

"I'll walk up with you."

And I did.

XV

In the waning moonlight, I switched off my running lights. Cuda Key was a mile or two ahead of me; a black hump of foliage and fortress on the gray sheen of roiled two-a.m. storm sea.

It had taken me about an hour and a half to get to Bahia Honda, running up on the rough Atlantic side, the *Sniper* ramming through the heavy roll of ocean like a country-boy fullback. I had run without lights until I got to the big bridge, letting the green bleep of the Si-Tex radar system lead me through the night. Just off Sugarloaf, the radar had picked up something big moving two miles or so off to starboard. I had shut the engines down, drifting, and took a good look through the Bushnell zoom scope. It sucked in all the available night light, revealing to me a big white cruiser heading shoreward from open sea. Like the *Sniper*, it ran without lights.

One more drug runner; one of the thousands that

operate under stealth and get rich in the Florida Keys.

On a different night, a later day, I might have waited and intercepted them. Because I was after them all. Every unmoraled son of them. And I would take them all, one at a time, or die trying. But on this night I had bigger game in my sights. I grimaced at the guy's good luck; promised him another meeting on another night, then started my engines and got back under way.

I had discussed tactics with Colonel Westervelt. And we had come to only one mutual conclusion: save for only the one or two obvious diversions I would have to set up to save lives, the rest I would have to play by ear. My only orders were to cause enough chaos so that, when the federal boys arrived with their warrants later on in the dawn, there would be enough unhidden and undestroyed evidence to put the lock on the Senator and his little army for fifteen years or more.

How I went about it was up to me.

I nosed *Sniper* around into the harboring shoals of Friend Key Bank and let her drift back on the incoming tide before dropping the big bow Danforth. When I had played out plenty of scope for the rising tide I set another hand anchor, then switched off the sweet bubble of twin GMC engines. In the sudden silence, I could hear muted voices coming across the water, from Cuda Key. People were awake on the island. People were moving about. But it couldn't be because of me. Something was up.

The storm was moving upon the chain of Keys now, swinging, as it usually does, around to the northwest: big gusts of wet wind followed by the flash of lightning, the momentary vision of rough green seas, and the flickering darkness of a westering moon beyond the stream of thunderheads.

It would be some nasty night.

I had a long swim. More than a mile. Normally, in those seas, it would have taken longer than I could allow. But with me I had brought the Navy's version of the Farallon-Oceanic underwater propulsion vehicle. It used two motorcycle batteries for power, had a 109,000-candlepower headlight, and could pull me along at nearly five knots. I couldn't use the headlight, but I needed the speed. Colonel Westervelt had outfitted me with the UPV, and with new Navy-issue mask and fins and snorkel. I didn't like them as well as my old stuff, but they would serve. He had offered me tanks, but I had refused. For one thing, I had them aboard if I needed them. But I didn't need them. As much as I had used scuba gear in the Navy, I still preferred free diving. I liked to be able to move underwater unencumbered. I liked to be able to shift quickly from water to land. That's what I had been trained to do. With tanks, it's hard to tell a good diver from a great diver. But free diving separates the men from the boys.

I rechecked my gear. RDX explosives, plus detonators. Cobra crossbow and plenty of shafts. Webber dart pistol with twenty-six darts—one of them loaded with the scorpionfish poison. Two thermite grenades. Wise underwater penlight. And my Gerber fishing knife—not built for survival, like the Randall, but it was razor-sharp and would do until I got the Randall back.

I took a rolling, windy moment, sitting on the teak boarding deck of the *Sniper*, to go over my plan of attack. And, after rearranging the order of the darts in the Webber, I spat in my mask and slid into the stormy water with the UPV.

It was a rough trip: high, windblown waves, a foul tide, and a nasty cross chop. The red four-second flasher blinked fitfully off the mud-and-coral shoals behind the bridge. I felt ready, alert, filled with adrenaline and a well-honed purity of purpose.

Revenge.

They would pay for killing my loves, my life. Those who didn't die would go to prison—Stormin' Norman would see to that.

And those who did die would die slowly, by my own hands.

I skirted the eastern edge of Cuda Key, away from the boat docks on the channel, then moved along the southern bank, the warm hum of the UPV covered by the roar of wind and waves.

I gained access to the island on the same mud flat, beneath the same cover of mangroves, as before. I checked the hiding place among the arching roots to see if my old gear was there. It wasn't. They had found it. And, I assumed, they had found my little Boston Whaler, too. And done what with it? Sunk it? The boat was impossible to sink—even if they cut it in half. I hoped it was tethered down at the boat dock. If it was, that would be my way back to the *Sniper*.

As I hid my UPV and stuck my mask, fins, and snorkel into the little knapsack, I heard the noisy step of someone approaching. I flattened myself against the warm muck of the mangrove bank and watched.

Two men with flashlights. They approached each other from opposite directions, both beyond the high screen of fence.

Guards. The Senator had posted guards. So, he suspected that someone was on to his little operation. And he was concerned enough to take military-style precautions. I looked forward to my meeting with the Senator. I wanted to look him in the eye.

I lay there and listened to them talk. They lit cigarettes, traded jokes, and laughed. Two drug-culture aces. I saw their stringy hair and bleak faces in the flare of the lighter.

"Stayin' dry, Romeo?"

"Shit no, man. Real bummer of a night. Senator's nuts, man. Gettin' paranoid or somethin'."

"I know where you're comin' from there, brother. Makin' us walk this fence all night long."

"Hey—got any little thing to set me right?"

"Some herb, *amigo*, that's it. That bastard Ellsworth is keepin' the C locked up nice an' tight until the boat's loaded. Like incentive or somethin'. Wants the brothers to work faster."

"Shit! I'm losin' it, man. Can't stand all this . . .

this *quiet*. Ain't nobody gonna try this island again. Not after they gave that last jerk the float test."

"Hah! *Float test*. You kill me, Romeo."

"Yeah—hey, give me one o' those numbers. Christ, packin' a gun like John Wayne, an' them goddam dogs stalkin' around like vampires or somethin'—I need a little somethin' to settle my head."

They rambled on for a few more minutes, shared a joint—the sweet musk of it drifting my way, then dissipating in the storm wind.

And then they moved away, in separate directions, each grumbling and moving the beam of his flashlight along the fence mechanically.

I crept up to the fence and pulled the strap of the Cobra crossbow off my shoulder. It is an amazing weapon, and it felt good to be holding one, ready for use, again. It is built of a light, tough alloy and has a draw weight of about 150 pounds. That means that the average man couldn't normally cock it more than once. But with the ingenious self-cocking device built in, a child could manage it. The small aluminum arrows can cover the length of a football field in little over a second and it has a maximum killing range of around three hundred yards. I checked the first shaft, making sure the rubber cap was in place and that I had added the single lead sliver for balance.

I gave the first one, Romeo, about fifty yards. He had stopped to light another cigarette. I lifted the Cobra, took careful aim, and squeezed the trigger.

F-f-f-f-f-iTT!

The blunt-tipped arrow hit him in the back of the head, and the young druggie dropped as if he had been magically deboned. His flashlight rolled down the slight incline to the fence.

A silent weapon.

Silent and deadly.

I checked on the other guard. He was about the same distance away, in the opposite direction. He hummed a tuneless little melody. He had heard nothing.

I added another shaft, cocked the Cobra, took aim, and fired. The arrow whistled toward him, quartering the strong wind and adjusting its flight just as I had planned. It dropped him in midstride.

He groaned once, then lay quiet.

I took out a stout length of rope and tossed it over the limb of the gumbo limbo tree. I pulled myself up into the tree, returned the rope to the big thigh pocket of my commando pants, then swung back down onto the ground, inside the confines.

I kept low, measuring my steps. I went to the first one, Romeo, took his pistol, shut off the flashlight. With shorter lengths of rope I tied him. I checked his heart. He was still alive. With surgical tape from my hip pocket, I gagged him. And then I moved back along the fence to the other fallen guard and did the same.

Poor little dopeheads. They would wake up with some kind of bad headache. A sudden flash of lightning revealed the two of them to me: sour-smelling shapes looking, in the white glaze of rain, like dirt heaps over a new grave.

They weren't dead, but they might just as well be. If it wasn't prison, it would just be more drugs and more drugs, until their brains rotted away.

They were not my real adversaries. They were really just victims; victims like Janet and Ernest and Honor. And Billy Mack. Victims of the big money boys; the human prey of the drug kingpins who remained safe and aloof, shielded by their wealth or their government positions.

But a handful of them weren't safe. Not tonight. Tonight, the hunters became the hunted. Tonight would become for them a stormy epic of revenge. Death for the brainrakers; death to the cocaine and heroin dream makers.

I retrieved the two aluminum shafts and moved on, toward the big house.

When I reached the base of the mound, I could see that the whole island was awake, mobilized.

Ten to fifteen men, rough-looking guys, black and white, carried boxes and paintings and small pieces of furniture from the house to the boat. Lights were on everywhere. This would be no easy job.

It crossed my mind that I should get to the caretaker, Jimmy, first. He had seemed like a pretty harmless old man, and I wanted to put him safely to rest, out of harm's way. And I was just about to make my move, to flush from the pepper bushes in which I was hiding, across the little shell clearing to his cottage, when I heard the low trio of growls, and the galloping footfalls of the Dobermans.

There was no doubt what they wanted to do. They wanted to rip my throat out; to get as much of me as they could before their master arrived and pulled them off.

But I was ready this time.

They charged at me from behind. I jumped to my feet and whirled around. The Webber dart pistol was already out, cool in my hand. In a flare of lightning, glistening in the steady rain, they looked like the hounds of hell: jagged teeth bared, ears pointed batlike.

There was no barking this time. They were ready to kill.

I shot the first two in rapid fire. Their momentum brought them crashing into me like eighty-pound sledges. I could smell the sharp musk of wet dog as they knocked me to the ground and sent the dart pistol spinning out of my hand.

And then the third one, the big red Doberman, was on me, slathering to get at my throat. I knocked the hot dead weight of the other two off my chest, and got to my knees just as the red one hit me. I felt his teeth snap deep into my left wrist, but I had him by the neck. I rolled backward, using his momentum, kicked him hard in the stomach, and kept a tight hold on his throat as he flipped over me.

Even in the steady roar of wind and rain I heard the gunshot snap as his neck broke. With one ghoulish whimper, the Doberman lay dead.

I got shakily to my feet. A spoon-sized chunk of flesh was missing from my wrist. It was bleeding— bleeding bad. Quickly I cut out a piece of pad from my old watch sweater, then wrapped my wound tightly with the surgical tape

It would do.

I took a deep breath, trying to settle myself. Two hundred yards away, the men working on the mound had heard nothing. They wore shiny wet rain slickers and bore their loads with dismal resignation. The rain was falling harder now, the lightning coming with loud regularity. Steam rose from the shoulders of the men, and it looked as if each of them were possessed by a slow, smoldering fire.

I recovered the dart gun in a blaze of lightning and headed for the caretaker's cottage.

He sat in the same old chair, beneath the same lamp, reading one of those slick porno magazines. He had the centerfold out. Through the corner of the window, over his shoulder, I saw the paper goddess looking strangely and pathetically alone, as all of them do. The old man flipped the page and studied the hand-scripted reproduction of her centerfold application. She was born under the sign of Virgo, her hobbies included all of the newest cult favorites, and her career dreams were torn between neurology and creative writing. She was nineteen years old, a year older than April, and already she was the surrogate lover of a million leering faceless men who would treasure her dearly in their loneliness—until next month.

I stayed close to the cottage and crept around to the door. Quietly, I swung it open and pointed the dart gun at the old man's chest.

"What the hell . . . !"

"Calm down, Pop. I'm not going to hurt you."

He held his hands up like a robbery victim in a film western.

"You can put your hands down, Pop. All I'm going to do is tie you up and gag you. Some people will be here in the morning to let you go. If you haven't done anything wrong, you have nothing to fear from them."

He put his hands down, reached for his old pipe, reconsidered, and eyed me warily. "Okay if I smoke?"

"Yeah."

He picked up the pipe, his hands shaking. "How'n the hell'd you get away? Thought Ellsworth kilt you fer sure."

"I managed. You don't have to know any more."

"Lord a'mighty, that knock he give you on the back o' the head that night was hard enough to kill a hog."

"I'll do the talking, Pop. I've got a score I want to settle. Where is Ellsworth?"

"Don't know an' I don't care. He's 'round here on the island someplace, yelling orders out like a slave owner. I quit 'em, I did. Quit 'em this afternoon. Told 'em I'm sicka their nasty ways. An' I meant it."

"Are they pulling out tonight, or tomorrow night as they had originally planned?"

He looked surprised. "Mister, you are a shrewd one. How'd you know that? Didn't know it myself, only guessed it. Heard somethin' about that creepy little Lenze fella gettin' arrested. Saw them loadin' the boat an' put two an' two together."

"And I hope you also figured that they would kill you before they left—because they will. If I don't get to them first."

He looked even more surprised. "Can't say as I did figure on it. But now that ya mention it, I guess you're right. Makes sense. They're an evil pair, them two. I tol' em that to their face, I did."

"How about the girl, Pop? Bimini. Is she all right?"

"The nigra woman? Hain't seen her in a day or two."

"What about the Senator? You think he'll be on the boat tonight?"

The old man rubbed his face and toyed with the pipe. "Doubt that seriously, mister."

"And why's that?"

He lit the pipe, hands now calm, blowing blue smoke across the room as the rain pelted down. " 'Cause the Senator hain't here, mister. Left in one of them heliocopters 'bout an hour ago."

XVI

The trick was to set up my secondary diversion so that I could get to my primary target—the big sport-fisherman that was being loaded and outfitted to take Ellsworth and his crew away.

The old man sat with his face to the wall, relaxed and ready to talk as I tied him. The wall was a peeling green, and there was a service-station calendar—big redhead with improbable bosoms—three years behind the times.

"Ropes too tight, Pop?"

"Nope. Jes' right. Don't really have to tie me anyway, mister. Got a sneakin' suspicion you're the law. Be glad to he'p ya. Frankly, I wouldn't mind givin' that bastard Ellsworth a slap or two myself."

I allowed myself a short laugh. "Pop, I need your help—but in a different way. Where did the Senator keep his important papers?"

"Couldn't tell ya. He'd never let me near that study o' his."

"That tells me quite a bit right there. Now, what about that small wooden building on the other side of the big house? Anybody live in it?"

"Nope—that's the toolshed. Nothin' in there but rats and some machinery."

I finished the last knot. "Pop, I'm not going to gag you. And you better not let me down. If Ellsworth or one of his boys shows up, you tell them three federal agents came in here and overpowered you. Got it? And don't mention me, no matter what."

The old man nodded complacently. It was as if being tied up was an everyday occurrence.

I slipped back outside. The storm pod was full above us now, and I took special care not to be seen in the white peal of lightning. The rain was warm on my face, and trees on the island, writhing in the wind, looked like huge living creatures, anchored in their agony.

I wanted to go to the house first. I kept thinking about the brave and beautiful woman, Bimini, who had saved my life. I kept wondering what they had done to her.

But I could afford no concessions to emotion. Not now. Not then. Not on any mission—ever. I had to follow my game plan.

Reluctantly I went in stealth, away from the house, down toward the boat docks. The men worked on; their monotonous lifting and passing, lifting and passing, captured in the yellow glow of a huge yard light. They carried smaller boxes now, wrapped in plastic against the rain. Drugs? Possibly. Ellsworth and the Senator probably wanted to make one last big score.

The docks consisted of a cement seawall, two long fingers of wooden pier, and roofed boathouse, beneath which was the racing boat. The big sportfisherman was secured between the two lengths of pier, well bumpered against the roll of sea. The men used the pier between the sportfisherman and the cigarette hull, loading via the starboard planking. There was no cover between the bushes near the cottage and where the swampy mangrove line started to the left of the second pier.

So I made a run for it. I had no choice. I tried to time the lightning; tried to time it just right. And then I made my move, running low with long, smooth strides. And when I reached the pier, I swung down beneath it and waited. Waited for some hue and cry. Or a gunshot. Or for the sound of Ellsworth's voice.

But there was nothing. Only the low laughter and conversation of the working men. They marched along, only fifteen or twenty yards from my new hiding spot, snatches of their voices coming to me only vaguely in the roar of storm.

"Ain't fit weather for man nor . . ."

". . . ought to about do it, huh, Gibson?"

"Hope so, man, hope so."

". . . an' what about that black bitch, huh?"

"Stick to them white girls, Ace. Stay on you own side o' da fence."

I strained to hear what they might have to say about Bimini. But I could make out nothing more. And when I was sure that they had not seen me, that none of them had caught even a glimpse of me, I reached into the knapsack and began putting on my mask and fins.

The area around the sportfisherman was well lighted. Very well lighted. There was a big floodlight above it, and it illuminated the water beneath it. The waves rolled and receded, jadelike and glistening. In its huge bulk, the sportfisherman barely moved.

I slid into the water, taking care not to let the sea crest knock me back into the barnacled pilings. In the flash of lightning, the mangroves that curved away from the pier threw weird shadows. I stayed close to the mangroves, pulling myself along in their cover. And when they reached a point, out and away from the pier where I knew the water deepened, I stopped and took ten good deep breaths, hyperventilating.

And that's when I saw it. Hidden back in a little cove, looking a fluorescent blue in the bright burst of lightning—my little Boston Whaler.

It was a good sign. A good omen. I had bought that solid little skiff for Ernest and Honor. It was the boat I wanted them to learn about the sea on. And now its discovery became not only a faster means of getting back to the *Sniper* when I needed to, it also offered fair augury for the approaching mission.

I almost smiled. It bounced and jerked above the spent waves like a toy duck. Fair sea, foul sea—a dependable little boat. It was almost like seeing an old friend.

It was a short sixty-yard swim to the Senator's sportfisherman. I got the RDX I needed from the knapsack and dove.

The lights of the boathouse guided me. They shimmered strangely on the pier, beneath the water, revealing silvered baitfish and the long, black stiletto forms of barracuda. I pulled myself through the water, using long, solid strokes of fin, my arms at my sides. There was no hurry. I had them now.

I surfaced beneath the dock at the stern of the boat. I could hear the loud creak of footsteps above me. Heavy men, heavy loads. The name of the sportfisherman, in golden letters a foot and a half high, blared out the boat's name: *Independence*.

So typical of the political hypocrite mentality—cover the vehicle of dirty deeds with glorious nomenclature.

It made me want to vomit.

I knew where I wanted to place the block of RDX. Under the skeg, beneath the engines. When the boat went, I wanted it to be useless for ever and ever; a wasted hulk to remind the Senator—and bastards like the Senator—that there are still some people you can't walk over. There are people who will fight back.

I submerged quietly and checked out the bottom. I wanted to do the job perfectly and with care—RDX is nothing to play around with. Cyclonite, military variety—one of the most powerful explosives of all. A partial block would do the trick and still leave the little Whaler, 150 yards or more away, high and dry. It would take the boathouse and probably damage the sleek blue death boat secured on the next pier—but nothing else.

I was concentrating so intently on fastening the RDX just right that it wasn't until too late that I realized I wasn't in the water alone.

Ellsworth was taking precautions, all right. Guards above the water. And below. And when the diver, complete with tanks and wet suit, grabbed me from behind, I suddenly understood what all the light was for. They had posted a night underwater patrol. Ellsworth hadn't been much of a SEAL—but he had worked with plenty of good ones. And he knew how to secure an area. I had to give him that.

The diver took me down, his arms locked around my throat. His plan was simple. He wanted to drown me.

I forced myself to be calm; to think. It was certainly not the first time I had been attacked underwater—in training or in actual combat. He would have a knife, of course. And I couldn't afford to make him use it. Even a lucky stab with my Gerber would only condemn him to a slow, bleeding death—long after he had cut my throat. He wanted to drown me? Fine. I would let him drown me.

I pawed at his arms frantically. I jerked and squirmed—but not hard enough to break free. And, after a half minute of that, I gave a final, convulsive heave and then went slack, letting a little, precious air bubble from my lips.

I was either some actor, or he was no critic—because he released his grip and began to pull me upward. And we had nearly reached the surface when I slid my Gerber out of its holster and jammed, with one smooth thrust, all eight inches of blade up through his throat, into his brain.

There was no violent death struggle from that diver. He folded as if anesthetized, and I carried him back down to the bottom, a black curl of blood following us. After a long, welcomed exchange of air from his regulator, I pulled him to a piling beneath the dock and tied him down with quick hitches, neck and legs. I took a few more deep breaths from his regulator, and then screwed off his air.

I didn't want anyone to notice that his telltale bubbles stayed, now, in one place.

The RDX was still in position. It hadn't been knocked loose by his attack. I secured it with a length of wire, considered adding another partial block for good measure, and then decided against it.

I surfaced once more beneath the dock for air, and then swam the sixty yards back to the mangroves underwater. The rain hit my face with an angular velocity when I surfaced. Stormy August night: sea and rain both as warm as blood.

It would be best to get Bimini out of the house—if that's where she was—before I started Diversion One. That I knew. In the dirty business of drug running, all witnesses, all competitors, all unwanted baggage, are disposed of as readily as picnic paperware. And, besides, entering the house now might give me a few minutes alone with Ellsworth. The few precious minutes it would take to rip his throat out with my bare hands.

I put the mask and fins back in the knapsack and took a short breather. The underwater struggle had brought my head injury to bear. There was a throbbing pain at the base of my neck, and I felt a little dizzy. My wrist, where the dog had bitten me, ached with every pulse of heartbeat. I checked my Rolex. They still didn't know I was on the island. And my mission wouldn't take long to complete now. I could take it. I was in pain—but a sweet, sweet pain it was.

I stuck the detonator to the RDX into my left thigh pocket and buttoned it securely. And in the momentary darkness, I scampered back toward the cover near the little cottage. A bright explosion of lightning sent the limb of a huge gumbo limbo crashing to the earth, not far from the boathouse. I saw the men duck reflexively.

"Why'nt we call it quits for tonight?" I heard one of them yell.

"Can't, brother. Can't."

"I say screw Ellsworth."

"Keep it down, man. He'll be coming down from the house soon. Might hear you."

"I don't give a shit if he does. Tired of this crap, man."

So, he was in the house.

The Senator's hulking fortress sat huge and well lighted in the pouring rain on the mound above me. The yellow rectangles of windows looked like peering eyes from my vantage point. I wanted to gain entrance to the house unseen, get Bimini, and get her to safety. And once that was done, I could go ahead with the operation—which would mean that, for a few minutes, I would have free access to the sportfisherman and then, later, be able to roam the house at will.

If everything went as planned.

And it would. I had plenty of time, now. Things were going smoothly. Very smoothly indeed.

I wouldn't have seen the guard on the porch had it not been for the lightning. Big man, dressed in black, with a full black beard. He held some kind of automatic weapon, cradled in his arms. The guard, in the strange light, looked oddly like a wax figure.

I readied the Cobra crossbow, stuck a shaft in it, and cocked it. And then I leveled the weapon, poised on the dark space of side porch where I knew he stood. And with the next white crack of lightning, I fired. I didn't see him go down. But I heard him.

Humph!

All clear.

I hustled up the mound, hugging the jungle of wet foliage. Little rivulets of rainwater swirled down the ancient shells, heading for the timeless rendezvous of sea. Before I reached the door, I stopped and looked in the window of the master bedroom. The

Bach played on in evidence of the island girl who loved the classics. But she wasn't there. No one was in the room. The covers of the bed were thrown back, revealing silk sheets. There was a half-finished bourbon on the hatchcover table.

She was up and awake. But where?

I went to the fallen heap which was the guard. I pulled him down off the porch and hid him in the bushes, binding and gagging him. I took his weapon and jammed a solid length of jasmine twig down the barrel and broke it off.

The person who tried to use that rifle again would be awfully, awfully sorry.

Carefully, I opened the door. Just cracked it enough so that I could look in. The cold force of air conditioning hit me full in the face. I was at the side hallway. Beyond was the entrance to the master bedroom, the ornate bathroom and sauna bath, and the Senator's study. A huge dark figure stood outside the study door, and I could hear muffled voices coming from within—muted laughter; something that sounded like a groan.

I considered taking the guard out with the Webber dart pistol. But that would blow my cover. Instead, I shut the door quietly, then ran around to the back of the house, hoping I could get a look inside the study window.

I could. And I did.

And what I saw made me sick. I hit my own thigh hard, punishing myself.

You have plenty of time, plenty of time, Captain Dusky

MacMorgan. And things couldn't be going more smoothly.

Sure, sure. Absolutely.

Sometimes my own stupidity dazzles even me.

Ellsworth stood within. Trim, thin, naked body in the process of getting dressed. I saw his hateful, feminine face, the thin girlish lips. And I saw the beastly look of conquest in his dark eyes, complete with animal glow of triumph.

He had just finished raping Bimini.

XVII

She sat bound to a heavy leather chair, her legs tied wide apart. She was naked, brown body looking frail and defeated in the white neon glow of the study lamp. Her dark breasts heaved, glistening with the sweat of Benjamin Ellsworth, and small streams of blood dripped down the corner of her bruised mouth, and down the thighs of her immobile legs.

A cigarette hung rakishly out of the corner of Ellsworth's thin lips. He looked at the girl, laughed derisively, and opened the door to leave.

Quickly, I pulled the rubber tip off an aluminum shaft, lifted the Cobra, and fired.

"Shit!"

Some great SEAL; some cold professional I was. In my haste I hadn't even cocked the crossbow.

And then it was too late. Ellsworth was gone, pulling the door closed behind him.

I was trembling with rage. Poor Bimini, poor little

island virgin. Her head lolled back on the chair pathetically, her eyes closed as if she wanted to make the world disappear. I lowered the crossbow and tried to figure out how to intercept Ellsworth. I didn't give a damn about my game plan now. I wanted to kill him and kill him *now*.

He would probably head for the sportfisherman. I had heard the men talking. They were just about loaded. So he would go out the front door. And I was just about to leave the awful vision through the window to meet him when I saw the study door open again.

It wasn't Ellsworth this time. It was the guard. A huge black man. I watched momentarily, hoping for some sign of sympathy; hoping the guard would cut her free and give Bimini her clothes.

But he didn't. He had something else on his mind. He shook her by the shoulders and touched her naked body roughly. Bimini opened her dazed eyes, saw the huge man, then half cried and half screamed, "Stay away from me, you bastard!"

The huge man grinned.

"Gonna give you somethin' nice, darlin'."

"No . . . !"

He turned away from her, facing the window, and dropped his pants. The awful grin still creased his face. And he died with that grin; a horrible, frozen leer.

The silver Cobra arrow shot through the window as if it were tissue paper, entered and exited the guard's heart, then buried itself in the wall.

F-f-f-tt—CRACK—thud—CRACK.

All in a microsecond.

The guard studied the tiny hole in his chest, like a bear studying a bee sting. He tried to push the sudden gush of blood back in with a big black hand, and then he fell heavily to the floor, still leering.

"Gonna give you somethin' nice, darlin'."

Right.

Bimini's eyes widened in surprise and horror, and she inhaled as if to scream—but then didn't. Her eyes swept the darkness beyond the window where I stood.

"Oh, Dusky," she whispered in agony. "Oh, God . . ."

I kicked the window out, unconcerned with the noise now. I whipped out the Gerber and cut the ropes, and she stood up painfully and clung to me.

"I knew you would come back. I couldn't let myself believe that you were dead."

I pulled a blanket, neatly folded, off the leather couch and spread it around her shoulders. She shivered as if she were suffering from hypothermia.

"The Senator—is he coming back, Bimini?"

Her eyes were glazed, the glaze of severe shock. "I just knew that you would get here, Dusky. And now you're going to kill him, aren't you? But you can't. You can't because you have to let *me* kill him—"

"Bimini!"

"And I think I know how I'm going to do it. I'll take a knife and—"

"Bimini!"

She shook herself and stared at me, as if waking for the first time from her ordeal. And then she fell against me, crying in long, sweeping waves of anguish. I stroked her short black hair. "It's okay now, lady. I'm going to take you away from all this. But first you have to tell me—is the Senator coming back?"

She shook her head, still crying. "No, no, he went off and . . . and left me with that . . . that *animal*. Dusky, he . . . he . . ."

"I know what he did, Bimini. And he'll pay for it. I swear to you, he'll pay. One more thing, Bimini— the Senator's private papers. Did he take them with him?"

"In his desk," she said, motioning. "I don't know."

I sat her down on the couch and went to the desk. It took about five minutes to find the one with the false bottom. I jerked it open—nothing. Nothing but my Randall knife. He had cleaned the place out when he left. Left for where? South America, probably; left with a bundle, never to return. Unless one Norman Fizer had reason to hunt the Senator down. And I would give him reason. Plenty of reason. A whole boatload of it.

I secured the knife in my belt.

"Where are your clothes, Bimini?"

She nodded toward a pathetic little heap of underwear beside the chair.

"Stay right here. I'll get some stuff out of your room."

I went out into the hallway. Someone, attracted by the sound of the breaking window, was coming. I pushed myself against the wall, praying it was Ellsworth.

It wasn't. Another of the drug flunkies. He was so surprised when I stepped out in front of him that he took a wide, flailing punch at me, the kind of punch that angry little girls throw. I hit him once in the throat, a good one, straight from the shoulder. He went down gagging and gasping. I didn't even stop to see if he would live or die. I got jeans, a wool sweater, and shoes from Bimini's closet. I took them back to her and, ludicrously, turned my back as she dressed. When she was ready, I took her out the side door and back down the mound.

The boat was loaded now. The big twin engines rumbled, muted in the wind and downpour of the storm. We crouched there by a sweet-smelling hibiscus bush, and I told her what I was going to do.

"It'll take about ten minutes, Bimini. Do you think you can wait?"

She nodded, looking me in the eyes. I couldn't tell if the water on her autumn colored face was rain or tears. "Whatever you say, Dusky. Just take me away—that's all I want."

When I was sure that it was safe, I hustled her across the clearing to the mangroves. We waded along the bank, back into the little cove where the Boston Whaler lay at anchor.

"Sit flat on the bottom of the boat. Don't mind the water—I'll run it out later. And don't lift your head up for anything, Bimini. There might be some bullets flying around after the first explosion."

When I was sure that she was comfortable, I waded back along the mangroves to the first pier. I could see the toolshed, beyond two big trees. It was about two hundred yards away on the other side of the mound, dimly lit at the outer edge of the big yard light. Ellsworth and his men were nowhere to be seen. The work done, they had all been driven into the boat or into the big house by the rain. I took out the Wise penlight and readied a shaft. I added the proper weights. It was not guesswork—I had done it before. Back in Nam. And when the shaft was properly weighted, I took out one of the thermite grenades. In Asia, I had had one true great horror— that of being wounded by thermite. It is terrible stuff. When it goes, it throws a white-hot flame, in excess of four thousand degrees. And the smallest fragment of it can burn through your skull, right down to your toes. I gauged wind and distance. Then I fixed the thermite canister to the tip of the shaft, pulled the pin, aimed, and fired.

Crack—wo-o-o-osh!

It looked like the wooden toolshed had just been hit by a meteorite. The entire back half of the island was illuminated by a hellish white light as the building burned.

"Hey . . . fire!"

"Get some extinguishers, man!"

"Someone tell Mr. Ellsworth that lightning or something hit the toolshed!"

They came running out of the boat and out of the house like ants from a damaged anthill. But, with the extreme heat, they couldn't get near the building. I wondered if Ellsworth would remember what thermite was like. And then I wondered if he had ever let himself get close enough to actual combat to find out.

When I was sure the fire had everyone's attention, I scrambled across to the next pier and climbed aboard the *Independence*. It was about forty feet of class fishing boat—like the ones you see in the exclusive yacht basin in Miami and Ft. Lauderdale. Mahogany and brass were all polished to glass; the latest electronics and nautical niceties. It was a craft decorated and outfitted to impress visitors, not to work. And that made it even more like the yachts of the big rich boys. She had probably been the vehicle of half a dozen real fishing trips, but a hundred cocktail parties. I felt sorry for her in a way. She was solidly built but misused through kindness—like a good hunting pup who is raised and, finally, ruined in the show ring.

The door to the forward salon swung back and forth in the wind. The cabin was empty. I moved across the color-coordinated carpeting to the forward berth. It was jammed with the boxes I had seen the men carrying. With my knife, I cut through the plastic and the cardboard to find a paper bag which read "North American Sugar, Inc."

Sugar?

I ripped the sack open, the white powdery contents spilling down on my rubber dive boots. I touched my finger to my tongue: an odd numbing flavor with the texture of baking soda. Cocaine or heroin—I didn't know. We hadn't covered narcotics in SEAL training. But it sure as hell wasn't sugar. I stuck three bags of it in my knapsack and then went through the drawers beneath the bunks. Clothes and food and supplies. That wasn't what I was looking for. I checked to see how the Senator's little army was doing. They were still busy. Real busy. The thermite had spewed over onto the main house when it exploded, and now that was on fire, too; the roof of the north wing was aflame.

I ransacked the galley and ripped the seats of the kitchenette open: nothing but foam rubber.

It had to be there someplace—but where?

It took me awhile, but I finally found what I was looking for. A metal waterproof case, shoved way back beyond the twin engines, in the bilges. I pulled it out, foul and dripping, busted the lock, and opened it wide. Neat bundles of cash, sealed in brown wrappers. Twenties, fifties, and hundreds. Used bills. I thumbed through two stacks. A little over a thousand in one, a thousand even in the other. There were more than fifty stacks. I stuck thirty of the stacks in my knapsack, resealed the rest in the metal case, and tossed it back into the bilges.

I was safely away when I blew up the boat. I had run along the pier, across the clearing to the covering mangroves. I flipped back the spring-lock cover of the detonator, pressed the button, and, after a micro-second pause, there was a tremendous *ka-a-BOOM* that shook the little island so completely that, for a crazy moment, I thought it might sink beneath me.

I put the detonator away. I took the Cobra cross-bow off my shoulder and crouched there in the shadows, waiting.

I doubted if the sinking *Independence* would bring Ellsworth out of hiding, but I hoped the money might.

But it didn't. Oh, it brought the others on a run. They came wheeling down the mound like kids on an Easter-egg hunt.

"Shit, man, what the hell's goin' on here?"

"Goddam place goin' nuts—hey, gotta be some cash on that tub!"

"Screw the cash, Jack. Save some o' th' stash—we all gonna be rich. Ain't nobody around to stop us!"

The *Independence* lay stern to bottom, bow high in the air, and the men swarmed aboard. She looked sadly like a huge dying animal.

If the sinking sportfisherman didn't bring Ellsworth on the run, then he knew. He knew that the thermite explosion was not an act of God and lightning; he knew that the floundering boat was not the victim of a poor fuel-ventilation system. He knew that something or someone was after him. And to find him, I would have to hunt him down.

I watched for him as I ran back up the mound toward the burning house; watched for the dark trousers and blue foul-weather jacket he had pulled on after raping Bimini. I strained to see through every flash of lightning, but he wasn't around. The roof

of the house was burning merrily, popping in the
weakening shower of rain. No one guarded the doors
now. The men were in happy revolt, each trying to
salvage his own future from the sinking boat. I
kicked open the front door, went in, and switched
on the lights. The ceiling steamed above me, the acrid
odor of thermite and burning shingles everywhere. I
went through the house a room at a time, one by one.

Nothing.

In the Senator's study, I took special care. I opened
the drawer with the false bottom, stuffed in the sacks
of drugs, and added ten stacks of cash. Stormin' Norman could run him down on income-tax evasion if
nothing else. The desk was built of sleek metal, and
the stone walls of the house would never burn. The
federal boys would find evidence enough—if they
looked for it.

After checking the cellar, I ran back up the steps,
outside.

Where? *Where?*

I had decided to check the old caretaker's cottage
when I heard the roar of the racing boat being
started. I couldn't believe it. I ran around to the front
of the house and, from the high vantage point of the
Indian mound, I saw it: somehow the boathouse had
protected it from the brunt of the explosion.

Ellsworth was at the controls.

His men were yelling at him. I couldn't make out
the words. A lanky kid with long, long black hair
tried to jump aboard, and Ellsworth shot him down.
The kid had his arms full of drug sacks, and the

white powder spilled over his bloodied face. The rest of the men stepped back in horror—and then ran, none of them taking the time to drop their booty.

The boat was already in motion when I shot. He was more than two hundred yards away, through the trees and down the hill. The stiletto-shaped boat wallowed as if about to sink as he pulled out, then he jammed the throttles forward and it struggled to plane—so, it had been damaged by the explosion.

I lofted the arrow. A tough shot—but I had killed men with tough shots before.

But I didn't kill Ellsworth.

The arrow left with a hiss, and, a second later he stiffened, sagged momentarily, and then disappeared into the darkness. I had wounded him. But how badly? No way of telling.

But there was one thing I knew for sure. I would find him. Maybe not on this night, maybe not the next. But his time would come. If he wasn't dying now, he would; die by my hands.

"I'll hunt you down like a dog, Ellsworth," I whispered, my words lost in the storm wind. "I'll hunt you down and make you beg—that I vow."

Bimini had followed my orders well. She didn't sit up until I called her name through the darkness.

"Let's get out of here, lady. I want to get you to a hospital," I said as I threw my gear into the little Whaler.

"Did you . . . did you kill him?"

"I don't know. I don't think so—but I wounded

him. I don't know how badly. He just took off in that big powerboat."

She put her arms around me and pulled herself close. Warm little island woman; the fear in her voice edged the brave front. "Are we going after him . . . now?"

"No. No way we could catch him. Another day, Bimini. I'll meet Mr. Benjamin Ellsworth on another day—if he lives."

It wasn't my imagination. She sagged with relief.

I pulled the stern-well plug, running the rainwater out as we went. Bimini snuggled close beside me while, behind us, Cuda Key burned. It threw an eerie light across the water: green and bile-like, as if all the evil of that place were being leached out by the August storm.

We talked softly together as we banged through the choppy night seas.

"I'm so sorry, Dusky. So sorry about what he did to me. I wanted it to be you."

"It doesn't matter to me, Bimini. Not a bit. When we're sure you're well, maybe we can take a little cruise. A . . . a sort of friendship cruise. I can't promise you love or lovemaking. I just know I need to get away. And I want someone along. Someone who isn't afraid to speak up when there's something to talk about, and who isn't afraid to say nothing when talk is unnecessary."

She kissed me softly on the cheek. "I would like that. And I understand. You need time, Dusky MacMorgan. That's what we both need—time."

XVIII

By the time we got back to the *Sniper*, Bimini had even managed to laugh a little. I wanted to cheer her up, to get her mind off what had happened. And trying to cheer her up actually cheered me up.

She didn't ask me what had happened back on Cuda Key. And I didn't tell her. A strange thing about war—and that's what my attack had been, war. It draws on a human psychological reserve that is buried deeply within us all. It has something to do with the kick of adrenaline, the sudden, insane dissipation of all reason. It prowls the dark side of our brains like a benign tumor, only to leap alive and to the forefront when the provocation is sufficient. And when that creature, war, comes to life, it brings us face to face with a being so malevolent, so horrifying, as to render mere words not only useless but loathsome. It brings us face to face with ourselves.

I knew the horror. I knew it well. And when the

killing is done, I had learned to let the warrior in me return to its terrible and temporary grave.

So I talked and joked, anxious to get that good woman to the hospital; to steal her away from this awful night.

The *Sniper* lay nearly invisible in the dark distance. And then it became a shadowy form. And then I could hear the gentle roll and smack as she danced on her ground tackle.

I brought the little Whaler up smoothly and lashed it to the boarding platform.

"I feel so good with you, Dusky. I don't think I need a doctor; honest."

"I won't hear another word."

"Maybe we could just rest here awhile." Her mouth opened in a wide yawn, and then melted into a sleepy smile. I could see her face clearly now. The storm had all but passed, and a flickering moonlight spread across the water and lay milky on her skin.

"You go below. There's a blanket in the port locker. Get it out, take your clothes off, and get dry. And then get yourself some sleep. I'll run us back."

"I might need some help—getting dry," she said, kittenlike.

And I knew what she was doing; what she needed. After her terrible experience with Ellsworth, she needed someone to show her that it could be good, that it could be right. Someone to show her the love of it before memories of her rape hardened in her brain and spoiled all bedroom love for her forever and ever. She needed me now, to love the nightmare away; now before it began to feed on her.

"Are you sure, Bimini?"

She fell against me, looking up into my face. "Are you? The time we need, Dusky—the time we both need is now."

I bent to kiss her full lips and felt, beneath the wool sweater, that her nipples had already hardened, protruding through the wide weave of the garment. Perhaps she was right. They had killed a part of me, and I had killed many of them. Maybe this was the way to say yes; to affirm my own existence.

I kissed her again, harder, alert for any sudden recoil or revulsion within her.

There was none. She pressed hard against me, finding the entrance beneath my watch sweater and sliding her hands over my wide chest.

"Dusky, are you sure?"

I lifted her up in my arms, my left hand on the firm mound of breast. "Yes," I said. "Yes, I'm sure."

What happened then occurred so quickly that I doubt if I will ever get it straight in my own mind. Flickering images tainted with fear and awful, awful disbelief. And the dreamlike quality of a nightmare.

Kisses and laughter interrupted by the unexpected flare of cabin lights.

A pallid, haunted face.

A gun.

A leer.

Ellsworth!

"My, my, my, aren't you two quite the romantic lovers this evening!"

I dropped Bimini to her feet. I kept shaking my head. It was the concussion, the dizziness. I had to be having a hallucination.

But I wasn't. Lieutenant Benjamin Ellsworth stood before me. With a gun. Again.

I had wounded him all right. The aluminum arrow protruded through his thigh. His wet pants looked even darker for the blood. His face was blanched. Beads of sweat glistened on his forehead.

"What are you staring at, MacMorgan?" Ellsworth laughed crazily. "You're the ones who should be gawked at. The thought of it: a pathetic circus orphan and an uneducated nigger whore exchanging sweet words of love. It makes me want to puke."

Shakily, he climbed the two steps to the fighting deck. Blood gushed from his shoe when he moved.

"What would your late wife say about that?" He threw his head back, cackling like a maniac. And he leveled the gun at my head when I took a step forward. "She wouldn't like it, would she? Nor would your two boys."

"Don't!"

It was Bimini. She wasn't trembling now. I had never seen a look of such stark hatred on any woman.

Ellsworth smiled at her. "Don't or you'll what?"

"Don't talk to him that way!"

He turned to me. "Look at this, will you? The big

man is letting a colored woman do his talking. How about that, MacMorgan?''

"I've got nothing to say to you, Ellsworth. If you're going to kill us, get it over with. But you'd be smart to let the woman live. You're going to need someone to take care of that leg—or you'll bleed to death.''

"Oh, this?'' He motioned grandly toward the arrow in his leg. "I assume this was a little present from you.'' He coughed and wiped the sweat from his face. "I must say that I was surprised to find your boat out here. I can't imagine how you escaped our last encounter. My own craft was sinking—damaged by another little gift of yours. I thought it wise to abandon it and take this vessel. And I would have— but for one thing. No keys. Hand them over, Mac-Morgan. Now.''

He wasn't thinking clearly. It was a mistake no pro would have made. No healthy pro, anyway. Had he been thinking clearly—thinking like the SEAL he never really was—he would have killed me and then taken the keys off my corpse. Only he wouldn't have found them. They were under the starboard berth. Back in the corner. Where I always hid them.

But he wasn't thinking clearly. And he did make the mistake. I reached slowly toward the big right pocket of the commando pants where the Webber pistol was concealed.

And by the time he realized his error, the dart gun was halfway up and out.

If Bimini had done anything else, he would have

recovered in time. If she had just stood by and looked on in horror—like most people—I would have died in my tracks; died with the satisfaction, at least, of knowing that Lieutenant Ellsworth was well on his way to bleeding to death. But she didn't wait. She didn't watch. She jumped toward him like a young lioness, her fingers raking even rows of flesh from his face.

The .45 roared and Bimini jolted backward and landed on the deck in a heap. She rolled over once, blood dripping from her head, groaned, and then lay silent.

Thud!

Ellsworth stiffened in surprise, dropping his weapon. I had shot quickly, not waiting until the Webber was level and controlled. And I had hit him in an improbable place. He grabbed his groin, eyes wide and filled with wonder. He knew about dart guns. And what he knew frightened him.

"What's . . . what did you shoot me with?"

I had him now. And I was going to make him suffer. "Poison, Ellsworth. The poison of a scorpionfish."

"No! You can't . . ."

"I can and I have." I took two steps toward him and kicked the automatic away. "I want to tell you about that poison, *lieutenant*. You'll be feeling it soon. There will be a numbing pain. . . ."

"Yes!"

"And then you'll go into convulsions. And then the numbing pain will become unbearable pain. . . ."

"Please!"

"Please what, lieutenant? I can't save you now. No doctor on earth could save you now."

He crawled toward me, one hand still holding his groin. "You've got to do something, MacMorgan. Yes—*you've got to* . . ."

He clutched at my pant leg like a little child.

"Can't . . . stand . . . pain. *Please.*"

"What about other people, you bastard? You think my wife, my boys, my best friend, or this woman enjoyed pain? And you killed them, you bastard! You killed them all!"

"Yes . . . I'm sorry . . . save me, MacMorgan . . ."

He stared up at me with horrible eyes. But I felt no pity. I kicked him away from me. "There's only one thing I can do for you now, Ellsworth. I can put you out of your misery."

"No!"

I turned away, as if to start the boat. "Then suffer, lieutenant."

"No! Yes, I mean *yes!*" He was crying now, bawling like a child.

"Beg me."

"My God!"

I stooped and lifted him by his foul-weather jacket to his feet. And I looked into his appalling eyes, holding him tight. "There's no other way, lieutenant. Two hours of dying or a split second of death."

He sagged, still crying. "Okay . . . I'm begging you."

The moment the words were out of his mouth, I

shoved him back and then pulled him forward into
the full force of the palm of my hand. It shoved his
nose up into his brain, and he died as I had promised. Quickly.

He was a foul and evil person, but still I felt sickened by it. Sickened by the sights and the sounds of
death, and his last pathetic minutes. I dropped him
down onto the deck and then, deliberately, I took the
Webber pistol from my pocket.

And then I fired it into the night, aiming at the blur
of chaotic universe. It was the death dart, the killer. It
was the dart with the real poison of the scorpionfish. . . .

XIX

On a Saturday in late September, I cruised the *Sniper* along the desolate point and white sweep of empty beach off Cape Sable. It was a flawless day: a world of soft blues and yellows; a world of sun and calm sea. And solitude.

The southernmost west coast of Florida is unlike anything else the Vacation State has left to offer. It is vast mangrove forests, trees eighty feet high, and dark tidal rivers and uncharted oyster bars where the tides have ebbed and flowed for a thousand years, known only to the snook and tarpon and redfish which hunt there. It is an immense sea and backcountry wilderness unblemished by the scars of the Florida epic: billboards and trailer parks, condominiums and fast-food stands and roadside attractions—the hallmark of progress and the idiocy of the Florida businessman.

It is a good place to rest.

A good place to disappear.

I nosed the *Sniper* toward shore, into the lee of Lake Ingraham Creek, far enough away to keep the bugs in the mangroves, but close enough so that it would be an easy swim to the desolate beach.

The woman had her back to me, naked and well oiled against the September sun. And when I gave her the word, she dropped the Danforth while I reversed the engines, churning the blue water, setting the hook. And then she turned to face me on the fly bridge; heavy thrust of now tan breasts, sweet glimmer of oil on body hair and perfect thighs.

"You want me to get you something cold to drink?"

She nodded and lay back down on the foredeck to bake in the sun.

Some woman. We had left Key West two weeks before; left to escape and rest and promise each other nothing. A boat trip to the wilderness is better than any hospital. Besides, I had had my fill of hospitals. And she had agreed.

So we had cruised across Florida Bay, stopping when we wanted to stop, swimming when we wanted to swim. She liked sitting on the deck with a book. I liked working on the *Sniper*: polishing and painting, trying to bully the horror back into hiding through manual labor. For the first week, we had been as shy and awkward together as children. If I saw her coming aft along the port walkway, I would back up and take the starboard walkway forward. When our eyes met unexpectedly, she would turn and look away as if there was something to see on the distant glaze of horizon. But slowly, through soft talk and laughter, the shyness dissipated, replaced by a growing, almost tangible sexuality. Janet, my Janet, was gone . . . and I would have to find a way of going on.

It happened on the eighth day. A twilight dinner of snapper, rice, and fresh lime, anchored in the clear shallows of Florida Bay. Sitting across from me, both of us flushed with the nearness of the other, I had found it impossible to eat.

"You're not hungry?"

"Guess not."

And when we both stood to clear the table, we bumped into each other. We turned and collided again. The cabin felt no bigger than a closet. She took me by the shoulders then and looked up into my eyes. I felt like I was on fire.

"Dusky, I . . ."

Before she had a chance to finish, I had kissed her. It was like the breaking of a dam. She couldn't get my weathered jeans off fast enough, nor I hers. It was the convalescence we both needed; an affirmation of love.

And God knows I had needed it. After the return from Cuda Key there had been the awful trip to the hospital. And then the meetings with Fizer; meetings and more meetings.

"You've done us a great service, Dusky."

"Sure, Norm. Sure."

"We've got plenty on the Senator—now it's just a

matter of getting him back to the States. The rest of his flunkies are already looking for lawyers. Except for the old caretaker. He was released and given protection. The prosecution will be using him."

"Fine, Norm. Fine."

Norm Fizer had looked at me, the concern obvious. "Look, Dusky, it's over. I know how it is—like back in Nam. But you can't let it eat away at you. So drop it."

And I had smiled; a bitter smile. "And you also know how hard it is to 'just drop it.'" And then: "Norm, I stole about twenty thousand bucks from Ellsworth's stash."

He nodded. "I know that. I wasn't going to say anything."

"And I got a money order and sent all but a thousand of it to Bimini's folks."

"I know that, too." He had stood and clapped me on the shoulder. "As far as I'm concerned, captain, the case is closed. Take a month or so off. Drink some beer; drink a lot of beer. Get roaring drunk and hunt down some big fish with that boat of yours. And I'll be in touch later—if you're still interested?"

"Yeah, Norm. I'm still interested."

So one night the girl had come down to the docks. She wanted a private audience. A two-week private audience. And I had agreed, not even daring to hope it would turn into a healing, loving cruise of hot sun and cold beer and idle, idle days.

I climbed down the ladder from the fly bridge and fetched the lady something tall and cold. And when

I took it to her, smiling at the fine nakedness of her, she rolled over, sleepy-eyed, her breasts flattening the tiniest bit beneath their own weight, and she held out her arms to me.

"This girl needs something more than Pepsi, captain. In the mood?"

I was.

I stripped off my shorts without haste, savoring my anticipation, and I lay down beside her, feeling the oiled buttocks lift at my touch, feeling her warm lips, soft, coiling her long silken hair in my hands. And when she slid herself up and onto me, joining us with a low moan of ecstasy, I whispered her name, feeling it sweet on my lips:

"Lisa . . . Lisa . . . Lisa-lee. . . ."

Here's an exciting glimpse of
the thrilling adventure that awaits you in the
next novel of this action-packed series

THE DEEP SIX

Underwater, in the angling tawny light of late afternoon, everything was gold. Flaxen sea fans undulated in the current that swept around the reef, and aureated and jewel-crested reef fish watched the naked woman as she reached beneath a pod of brain coral and pulled out a spiny lobster. It was a big one—enough for her half of the supper we would eat back on my thirty-four-foot cruiser, the *Sniper*. Drifting above, mask in the water, breathing easily through my snorkel, I watched the naked woman with delight. Even she appeared gold in that strange afternoon light; a tenuous light that seems unique to the open sea, and to the reef islands far, far off Key West. It is a light that does more than illuminate—it seems to melt and liquefy, gilding everything it touches: the Australian pines and coconut palms that leaned in windward strands on nearby Fullmoon Cay; the long sweep of white beach on Marquesas

Keys; the blue and then orange expanse of open sea as the sun whirled toward dusk, setting behind the Dry Tortugas. And the woman, too. Drifting above the reef, I watched her slow ascent. Her blond hair streamed behind her in a long veil. After a month on my boat, her body was bronzed and trim, and the bikini strips on chest and hips appeared as pale geometrics upon her golden nakedness. She winked at me as she stroked toward the surface, holding the lobster like a prize.

Gold, gold, gold.

Later, it would return in my memory as a prophecy. An augury of the future. That's the way our minds work. Something happens, and our brains scan the past for omens. It's a human compulsion: search for order in a universe that, at times, seems to be anything but orderly. A friend dies and, in our minds, his last words take on portentous significance. We are involved in an accident, and we remember that "something" told us not to take the trip. Now it was golden light on a golden sea and in less than two hours it would take on a whole new meaning.

I watched the girl. She wore only mask, fins and snorkel. Oxygen bubbles, clinging to her blond triangle of body hair, looked like little pearls, and her breasts moved with heavy, liquid weight. Her beauty, the reef, and the afternoon light filled me with a strange yearning.

"Hey! Look what I've got!" She pulled the mask off her perfect face, laughing with delight.

"I know what you've got—it's hard to miss."

She slapped at me with mock outrage. "Oh, you! I'm talking about the lobster. Isn't he a beauty?"

He was indeed. A beautiful crustacean, the Florida lobster. No claws, but with sharp spines between their eyes that can needle through heavy cotton gloves. And because of that, this woman, Lisa-lee Johnson—Lee, I called her—hadn't caught one the whole trip. But she wasn't one to give up. Some afternoons she would come back from diving with her hands perforated, then sneak off to the first-aid kit to doctor herself in private. She never complained and I never let on that I knew. And the next day she would go back down for more. Until now. Finally, she had caught one. And it was a beauty. A two-pounder, easy. Her blue eyes gleamed victoriously as she dropped it, squeaking and kicking, into my dive bag, and we swam together over to the little Boston Whaler I had hauled along behind my *Sniper.*

"And what about your supper?" She sat naked on the low gunnel of the thirteen-foot boat, her blond hair hanging down in a thick wet rope, dripping water on her upturned breasts.

"Ah . . . supper , . . oh, yeah. . . ."

"Your mind seems to be someplace else, Dusky." She grinned bawdily.

"Dressed the way you are, woman, I find that my thoughts are on anything but food."

The smile left her face, and a new look came into her blue eyes; a heavy, sleepy look with which I had become very familiar over the past month. It had been a good month. A month of sun and fish and clear water; a month of aimless cruising, and then, love. In our own ways, we were both healing. Lee had separated from her domineering husband. And for me, only two eternal months before, the pirates, the ruthless ones, the money-hungry drug runners, had blown my life apart. A little ignition bomb in the trunk of our old blue Chevy. How were they to know that I wouldn't be the one to start it that awful August night? And why should they care that my beautiful wife, Janet, and my twin boys, Ernest and Honor, had been killed instead?

Well, I had made them care. And the few I had allowed to live would regret it until their own dying day.

So, when I was done with them, I had returned to my dock in Key West to find this woman, Lisa-lee Johnson. I had come to know and admire her when she and her husband chartered me and my *Sniper* for a day of fishing, and I had welcomed her tearful request to cruise alone for a few weeks. She wanted to cruise to think. And I wanted to get away so I wouldn't have to think. When we left Key West and headed across Florida Bay, we were two strangers filled with our own private horrors. The first week had been one of nervous laughter and averted glances. Neither of us was interested in love—just companionship. I had seen too much recent death and had done too much killing to want to be alone. And she—well, she seemed to be looking for a man strong enough not to try to hurry her into the sack; a man she could talk to and depend upon while she made up her mind about the husband she had left behind.

But it seemed inevitable that we would become lovers. I had known from our first meeting that there was a strong sexual awareness between us. You know it instinctively, and it has nothing to do with coy exchanges and suggestive remarks. And when we had finally kissed, it was like a dam breaking. We couldn't get each other's clothes off fast enough. We couldn't touch each other enough. We couldn't satisfy each other enough.

"Oh, Dusky, is it so awful that I want you this way . . . ?"

"No, Lee. No . . ."

It was an affirmation of the things we had left behind; an affirmation of the new lives each of us would have to find. And afterward, we would talk: long, rambling, self-indulgent conversations, telling each other everything. We didn't talk like lovers—nothing about our combined plans and hopes for the future. We talked like best friends. We soothed each other and tried to bolster sagging egos and shattered dreams.

It was harder for me to talk than it was for Lee. I find it difficult to stick more than four words into a sentence, and more than one sentence into a paragraph. I've always been quiet. Not shy, just quiet. My wife used to kid me by calling me Captain Stoic. But finally, with Lee's gentle help, the words started pouring out. When someone you love dies, you first feel outrage, then remorse, then guilt. I had been through the remorse and outrage—nearly a dozen men died in the flare of it. And Lee had helped me reason the guilt away.

"I just can't figure out the why of it. Why did that woman and those two boys have to die?"

"Dusky, you told me once when we first met that for some things there are no reasonable explanations. There is only acceptance. It's happened. Accept it. And go on."

So we had worked our way across Florida Bay, up into the Ten Thousand Islands wilderness on the mainland west coast, and then back across open ocean to the Dry Tortugas, and then here, to the Marquesas, working our way along to Key West and the end of the trip. The autumn days were hot and calm; perfect days for slow love and cold beer and talk; golden autumn days.

Golden.

Lee sat on the gunnel of the Boston Whaler, her long legs draping over into the clear water. And when her eyes softened, I leaned and kissed her, tasting the salt on her lips, feeling the warmth of her mix with the warm sea wind that wafted across Fullmoon Cay to the reef over which our little boat was anchored.

"And what about your supper, captain?" She smiled at me impishly. I was close enough to her face to see the little bronze flecks in her blue eyes.

"I've got my sling. I'll go down and shoot a snapper—later."

"Later?" She smiled and kissed me.

"Later."

Naked, she stretched back on the mahogany seat of the Whaler, her eyes closed, her arms folded behind her head.

"You're cold from diving."

"Hum . . . so I see."

A bottle of coconut oil sat on the little console, warm from its day in the sun. "This might help." I began to massage it into her skin, enjoying the scent of it, and the vision of this lovely blond woman.

"You seem to be concentrating on limited areas, captain."

"Certain parts of you look colder than others."

She opened one eye, squinting at me. "And parts of you look anything but cold."

I put down the coconut oil and leaned over her, kissing her body, caressing her outstretched legs, feeling her breasts full against me, and then—and then she pushed me away, giggling vampishly. "Your turn to suffer, MacMorgan!"

"What?"

Oh, she made me suffer. With the coconut oil. And her hands. And her lips. And had she made me suffer a minute more, I would have attacked her then and there. But she didn't. Instead, she grabbed one of the yellow Dacor scuba tanks, and her mask and, with a short laugh, jumped into the clear water. And I soon followed.

Beside the reef was a pocket of sand. Iridescent blue-and-green parrot fish scurried away at our approach, and the woman lay back in the sand, motioning for me. And there, three fathoms down, we made slow love. Beneath clear water, experimenting with the new weightlessness and the variations it allowed, we coupled in a stream of bubbles, drifting with the sea. Barracuda looked on, stern as maidenly aunts, and yellow-eyed groupers peered at us strangely from their rocky hideaways. I was filled with my passion for Lee and my love of the sea, but I also felt a sweet-sad ache, because I knew that she would be leaving me upon our return to Key West, and that I would probably never see her again.

Afterward, Lee climbed back on the little Whaler to bask in the sun and I took my sling down to the reef alone. I wore no tank. Even after three tours of duty in Nam as a Navy SEAL, I still preferred just mask and fins. No regulator to worry about. No metal fittings to konk you on the back of the head. When I am in the water I love the freedom of unhampered motion. Besides, spearfishing with a tank is one of the most pathetically unfair "sports" imaginable. The poor fish doesn't have a chance. I dove down to the top of the reef, then worked my way along a shelf of coral in about twenty feet of water. Small snapper and yellowtail moved away from me in perfect, orderly sheets, as if one mind controlled them all. I knew exactly what I wanted for supper, and I moved away from the reef to find it, propelling myself along the bottom with long, smooth leg strokes. A big cuda followed me, drifting alongside effortlessly. He was a five-footer, easy, and mossy-

colored with age. I didn't mind. If he wanted the fish
I shot, he was welcome to it. I would just get another.

I was after a nice hogfish, and I finally saw one
beneath a sea fan in a clearing of coral sand. At first
he was a pallid gray in color, but at my approach he
flushed a bright nervous crimson, the black spot at
the base of the posterior ray vivid. It was a beautiful
fish, about a six-pounder, and I took him cleanly with
a shot through the head. He fluttered briefly on the
free shaft, then fell still—and that's when I realized
something other than the barracuda had been following me.

Attracted by the death vibration—or the earlier
love vibrations—a huge open-water mako shark
came slashing across the reef, its massive pointed
head swinging back and forth as it vectored in on
me and the dying hogfish.

Sharks and I are not exactly strangers. You won't
meet a SEAL who hasn't had some kind of encounter
with one. SEAL—sea, air and land commandos, the
toughest of the tough and the roughest of the rough.
And we just spend too much time in the water, day
and night, to miss. For me, it was a night swim long,
long ago on a training mission in the Pacific, one of
those freak occurrences: a big dusky shark that
wasn't supposed to be in those waters, and sure as
hell wasn't supposed to attack. He left me with 148
stitches in my side and a new nickname. It was some
scar. But strangely, Lee Johnson had come to be fasci-
nated by it, paying it special, tender attention in our

lovemaking. At any rate, I didn't want or need any more scars. I already had more than my share.

That mako was a beautiful creature: bright blue and then cobalt; a massive ten or eleven feet in length and probably weighing half a ton. The smaller species of shark don't bother me. They really don't. You learn to live with them. Besides, their instincts tell them to eat fish, not people. Believe me, if sharks ever got a taste for human flesh, there wouldn't be a saltwater beach on earth that was safe. But this mako was big enough to break all the rules.

The reef that had been alive with fish was suddenly still. They knew. This was more than just another big shark—this was a big shark feeding. He came toward me, his head slicing back and forth like a radar antenna. From the leg sheath, I drew my Randall attack-survival knife—the good-luck charm that had saved my life and had taken others more than once. But against this fish, it would be no more lethal than a bee sting. I drew it only as a prod. If it decided on me as supper, I could only try to jab its pointed snout and hope to scare it away.

I had been down a long time and was almost out of air. But I couldn't afford to try to surface. Sharks like dangling arms and legs. I thought about Lee back on the little Whaler, and I prayed that she wouldn't choose this moment to dive in and cool off. I watched the mako drawing closer and closer. He looked like a two-man mini-sub with fins and dead yellow eyes. I clung to a chunk of staghorn coral, and when he passed me the first time, I felt my legs drawing up behind me, swept along in his powerful wake. He had been close enough to take me in a bite.

But this mako, big as he was, had no interest in breaking the rules this day. He circled me once more, and still I hung motionless. Then, in one lightning swoop, he opened his brutish jumble of teeth, took up the hogfish, shook the spear free, then bolted back toward the reef, his head still jerking, his tiny brain still fixed on feeding. I didn't give him a moment to reconsider.

I surfaced on the side of the Whaler away from the reef and jumped into the boat with one kick of my Dacor TX-1000 Competition Class fins. Lee was in tears, still naked, but trembling.

"God, Dusky, I saw him coming . . . I kept screaming at you, but you never . . ."

She fell against me, crying.

As I started the Whaler and powered us back to my cruiser, Lee, wrapped in a blanket, leaned against me. I made jokes; I got her laughing. And I waited for the fear to catch up with me. That's the way it happens when you've had a close call—the fear doesn't come until later.

But it never arrived. Why? I wondered. And then I thought I knew: compared with the murders of my family and my best friend at the hands of the drug-running pirates who will forever operate in the Florida Keys, death in the grips of a creature so magnificent as that mako seemed pure and compelling.

My sleek charterboat was beautiful in that strange afternoon light. It is painted a deep night blue, with the words

Sniper
Key West, Florida

painted in small white script on the transom. It looked black against the soft blue of calm sea and against the backdrop of the island's sweeping white beach. We puttered up and I tethered the Whaler off on a long line, tossed out a small stern anchor, and then climbed aboard to receive the second shock of the day. We were not alone on the boat.

A gnomelike man stood on the deck. Gifford Remus. Old as he was, he looked at me with the same submissive uneasiness as always; the face of a little kid in the audience of some idolized big brother. And what he held in his gnarled hands brought all the saffron omens of sunset into sharp focus.

He smiled a wondrous smile, eyes wide, then held out a six-foot length of old Spanish chain.

It was made of pure gold.